A SINGULAR MAN

EMMANUEL BOVE
A SINGULAR MAN

TRANSLATED FROM FRENCH
BY DOMINIC DI BERNARDI

THE MARLBORO PRESS
MARLBORO, VERMONT

First English language edition.

Copyright 1993 The Marlboro Press, Marlboro, Vermont.

Translation copyright 1993 by Dominic Di Bernardi.

Originally published in French under the title
Mémoires d'un homme singulier
Copyright Calmann-Lévy 1987.

The publication of the present volume has been made
possible in part by a grant from the National
Endowment for the Arts. The costs of translation have
been met in part by a subvention from the French
Ministry of Culture.

Manufactured in the United States of America

Library of Congress Catalog Card Number 92-62857

Clothbound edition: ISBN 0-910395-94-2
Paperbound edition: ISBN 0-910395-95-0

CONTENTS

A SINGULAR MAN

RICHARD DECHATELLUX

It is not some story that I propose to tell. I haven't the
patience for that. This is too grave a moment. What should
I do? My God, what should I do? The paper bag I hooded
over the light bulb is scorched. I have been sitting at my
table for two hours already. It was raining hard outside.
Now I no longer hear anything at all. The stars may be
shining in the black sky. My, how solemn I am! By what
right am I adopting the tone of one who is suffering? Oh,
let's not bother ourselves hunting for an answer.

The days had gone by one after the other, each identical to
the last, for four years, four whole years. How could I have
let time trickle away like this? How could I have said goodbye to all dignity? I had got to the point of spending fourteen hours, sixteen hours in bed, of letting the bells and
chimes of noon find me standing before my wash basin. It
is unbelievable. Once dressed, I would lunch in a small
restaurant behind St. Sulpice, two doors down from a shady
hotel. The number of jokes I've heard cracked about this
neighborhood! Just think, a by-the-hour hotel for lovers
two steps from a church! I would linger at table. It was
never I who fought to catch the waitress' attention. My
obliging nature was established with all the habitués. Lit-

tle by little they had developed the practice of entrusting me with all sorts of errands. Howsoever foreign the place may be, wherever we take up our abode we end up with as many obligations there as in the bosom of our family. I would strike up friendships and have fallings-out with people who meant nothing to me. Everything so transpired that I seemed to owe allegiance to the group that I was part of without knowing why.

To give you an idea of the kind of events that absorbed my attention, I shall relate a minor incident. For a long time the owner of my hotel had been planning to remodel. Each passing week brought in new estimates, schemes dreamt up by new contractors. Perplexed, he would consult me. He was afraid—and I couldn't blame him—of getting in over his head. "You might do best to wait for more favorable circumstances," was my invariable advice to him, for all I asked was that he keep the place in repair. I had no money. I foresaw that with renovations the tone of the hotel would rise a notch. I would be expected to follow suit. Initially, they would take into account that I was a customer of long standing. But later on?

"What would you say if, for a start, I just had the place repainted?"

"That's not a bad idea. But if I were in your shoes, I'd wait until I was able to have all the work done at one go. I take the liberty of telling you this because you're asking my advice."

"You're probably right," he answered in a manner hinting at respect.

However, the next day, the painters set down their paintbuckets in the vestibule.

On the day of the letter I got in late. I had the feeling I would not be able to go to sleep. I wanted to talk, to be amongst people, but it turned out that everybody had something to do. At the restaurant the customers had left earlier than usual. There was no one in the lobby of the hotel. The Odéon theater, two or three of whose columns were visible at the end of the street, was closed that night. I went back out. On rue Cujas there was a café that extended a good way in from the street, sometimes I would run into familiar faces there. But the lights in the back room were not even on. What great disappointment over such a trifle! That was when I made the effort to accept my aloneness, to give its proper importance to the relief a human presence might afford me. I would wait for the next day to come. I would do some reading. I would smoke some cigarettes. I would lay familiar objects out around myself. I already had a picture of the lonely man I was going to be in my hotel room. He was not without a certain grandeur. However I did not decide to go home. I opened the doors to other cafés. They had turned, on that particular night, into bourgeois doors. They were not to be jerked shut behind you. Until now I had never suspected how fragile they were. People turned around to see who had opened them. And the rain kept coming down tirelessly, invisible in the darkness. "But why is going to bed more than I can face?" I cried out.

Eventually I spotted a certain Cyprien, a sad person in search of an audience. He was standing in front of the bar, holding forth. The Rights of Man. Off with Their Heads, and No Long Speeches. His country was waiting for him. From time to time he broke off in order to sing a few bars from the Carmagnole. I felt at such loose ends that I walked up to him, all ears, ready to take him seriously. He fell silent.

"What did your father used to do?" I asked in the hope that such a personal question might snap him back to reality.

"You're acting chummy with me now?"

He raised his voice, called on the cashier to witness my lack of respect. We had been bumping into one another in that part of town for the past three years.

"Doesn't seem to me we've ever been on familiar terms, *not to my knowledge,*" he declared solemnly.

"What a fool!" I muttered on my way out.

"What did you say?"

He followed me to the door. I watched him for a few moments, looking at him through the glass. I wasn't there anymore but he was going on with his insults and his threats. Sincere indignation, ah yes, I know all about that. Then I walked away. The falling rain scissored the lights. I pressed my five spread fingers to my throat to keep my overcoat collar up around my neck. I thought of that bare hand of mine gleaming like some star within the strangeness of my appearance. It was only ten-thirty. I walked down boulevard Saint-Michel. "Racing finals, all the racing finals," the newspaper hawkers were shouting. The finals? Could it be that there were people who had not yet heard them, who had not had time to buy a paper?

This lot that had been bestowed upon me, what a singular one it was! In my mind arose an image which, that Sunday evening, seemed to fit my situation exactly. Could I not visualize myself as that racer, a cut above the rest but given a handicap it never surmounts, so that it comes in sixth for example?

I finally decided to go back to my hotel. Nobody was at the desk, or rather, yes, back there was that stupid chambermaid who mounts guard whenever her employers are away, and to whom it does not occur to take advantage of the trust placed in her in her in order to give herself some importance. They had forgotten to shut my window. It had rained into the room, and the droplets on the wooden floor

robbed me of the sensation of intimacy I had been await-
ing.

Fortunately, for three weeks I had had a pleasant neighbor, an Austrian. I noticed light under his door. And actually I think his name was Nachtmann. I felt an urge to
knock. But up until now we had exchanged hardly more
than a word or two, and it could be that he wasn't alone.
The only thing I had heard him say—and the words were
rhythmed with the care that denotes the foreigner—was
"Please, monsieur, after you." Even so, to make his acquaintance was very tempting that evening. I would have
rapped discretely. Once. Once more. A third time.

"Who's there?"

"Your neighbor."

"What neighbor?"

"You know, the man to whom you said, 'Please, after
you' the other day."

He would have opened the door. I would have offered
some childish excuse. Matches. I would have apologized,
we would have talked, and between us fellow-feeling would
have come into being.

All that was ridiculous. I locked my door. Sleep, that was
what I was going to have to do. Nachtmann must be alone
on the other side of the wall. No sound of voices. From
time to time I heard him tapping his pipe. Oh hotel-owner,
'tis well that you do not hear him, you who have shortly to
cope with so many expenses. Then he started pacing. What
kind of work did this man do? What were his ambitions in
life? Weren't they too lofty for him? Perhaps he's a doctor
fresh out of school, or a journalist. Better that I never speak
to him. I felt ashamed. He had a job. He was young. He
believed in himself. I wouldn't be able to hide from him
that I had been living in this hotel for four years. He would
have smiled politely, but what scorn deep in his heart!

I took off my overcoat, then my hat. I shut the window. I checked to see that the objects belonging to me were all in their places. It was a habit I had. All my habits were waiting for me. They had followed me into this room. They had grown more numerous with each passing year. Yet it would take very little to enable me to be free of them. All it would take would be one event that removed me from everyday life. I put off going to bed. I had to stay dressed in order to move about, to walk, to defend myself. What was there then that had me so on edge tonight? Richard's letter. Richard (what a suggestive first name!) asked me to put my visit off for two weeks. *Two weeks!* "His schedule's not all that heavy, *not to my knowledge!*"

I drew shut the curtains. I was tired of playing this role of the person whom you sometimes glimpse from the street walking to and fro in his room, heedless of all others.

I got into bed. But I couldn't fall asleep. Richard's letter filled me with an uneasiness which became torture once I turned the light out. In the end, I had to get up. I read the letter over again. It was four lines long. "I don't have time to see you this week nor next. I'm very busy. Let's put off your visit for two weeks. Kindly come for lunch on that Monday the 17th of December." The lines were undated, unprefaced by any friendly salutation, and unsigned. Not just any Monday, but *that* Monday the 17th. Something determined in this letter's tone suggested an evolution unknown to me. Was the darkness accountable for this? My thoughts grew increasingly muddled. All that I was, all that I possessed, I owed to Richard Dechatellux. If he had discovered some means of getting rid of me, was I about to relive the appalling moments I had already been through? Given the late hour, and the fact that after all nobody depended on me, I went back to bed. After a few instants I fell asleep.

*   *   *

I woke up amidst silence. I had heard neither the humming of the electric vacuum nor the street noises which when coming in through opened windows kept the chamber-maids from responding to buzzers pursuing them from floor to floor. Noon was approaching. Right away I thought of the letter. Far from restoring the incident to its proper pro-portions, daylight made it appear to me even more serious. I recalled what I had learned about the way incidents come about. As a younger man I would have thought that ties like ours could be undone only over a period of time. Rich-ard would have handled it tactfully. Were he to cut me off it would only have been after investigations and prepara-tions. Presently I was finding out that you don't necessarily inch your way toward an explosion. The oldest friendship can be broken off abruptly, without an explanation, even without a reason. And while dressing, I considered the pointlessness of my worrying if everything was now over and done with.

Although our relations were those of two members of a family, I didn't dare call on Richard uninvited. Did his letter authorize me to overstep the rules? It was possible, after all, that I had misconstrued it, that I had detected in those four lines a meaning they did not contain.

Nevertheless, once I was ready I got the idea to go for a stroll past the house where he lived on rue de Rome. The weather was gray. The owner of the hotel was in the hall-way. Ever mindful of improvements, he was wondering, as he stood before the partition to a little office, whether re-moving it might not damage the adjoining walls. Ordinarily I would stop. I was the only guest who indicated any in-terest in all those questions. He never dreamt that this was pure kindness on my part. He believed—and I do indeed wonder how he could have so deluded himself—that I attached as much importance to beautifying the hotel as he did. "Once this partition's been removed," he said to me, "the lobby will be larger." So absorbed was I with my worries that somebody else's problem had never left me so untouched. I barely responded. But as soon as I had gone a few paces down the street I felt something extraordinary. Dread. It was dread. I had just realized that I was going to pay dearly for my indifference, that Heaven would not fail to have its shot at me. And I almost retraced my steps.

I boarded the bus that runs between place Saint-Michel and the Gare Saint-Lazare. The approach I had in mind was making me feel better. For hadn't I imagined that Richard had fled, that the chief purpose of his letter was to allay my suspicions, to slow my inquiries, to place me before a fait accompli? I wanted to see his apartment windows, make sure his shutters weren't closed, that the carriage entrance stood open, that traffic was continuing normally in the rue de Rome, that the local shopkeepers were again waiting on their clientele, that nobody, in the vicinity of the house, appeared to have anything up his sleeve.

It was one-thirty when I got to the restaurant. Berthe—a first name long since out of fasion—was sitting amid my usual tablemates. She joined me for lunch every rare now and then, maybe once a month, and always unannounced. She would arrive late. I would almost always be having my coffee. I would get up in order to sit with her off to one side. This time the opposite occurred.

After a few seconds of conversation, she remarked: "Those friends of yours are as nosy as concierges!"

"How so?"

"They wanted me to tell them who you are, what you do. I'd say that's about the limit in tactlessness, wouldn't you?"

Try as she did to appear sincerely shocked, I suspected that Berthe had not risen to my defense with any special ardor. Her loyalty could only have been that of a woman who was once your mistress, and who is nothing but a friend now. I didn't so much as bat an eyelash. It was all one to me. For Berthe and the others I felt nothing but indifference. They were free to run me down if they felt like it. Moreover, tattlings do not really affect us. However great the ill-will that we feel being directed our way, it almost never strikes home.

"Do you know what intrigues them most?" she asked.

Berthe and I had done some scheming together. What schemes they had been, my God! Their source had been the lowest form of selfishness. To be in a position to carry them out we had not shrunk from plotting to jeopardize others' interests, from causing harm to elderly people. But before going ahead with them, we broke up.

I scrutinized Berthe. She had forgotten what the excuse of being together had permitted us to imagine. She had forgotten, whereas I remembered. In this one fact lay all the difference between us. So then, was it not natural that she now be playing this apparently devoted role of the person who listens to what the adversary says in order to betray him afterward?

"It's your means of existence," Berthe went on. "I told them you received money from your family. I could say that, couldn't I?"

"Why couldn't you say it? You know perfectly well that it hasn't the slightest importance."

We left the restaurant and I said goodbye to Berthe. She had been a distraction. Nevertheless my thoughts kept returning to Richard. My rue de Rome expedition had only temporarily reassured me. I went into a post office and telephoned Richard. "Who's calling?" the maid asked. "Don't hang up, don't hang up—" Somebody had answered the phone. That was all I needed.

Three days passed. To me they seemed interminable. Nothing irritated me so much as waiting. I had waited, in my life, for too many events, events that were to take months to come to pass, even years. All that was now over. I no longer awaited anything or anyone. I had stopped making plans. I had stopped making appointments. Berthe, on parting, would always ask me to tell her when we were to meet next. "Come by whenever you like. It will be clear enough if I don't happen to be in." Only my relations with Richard remained punctual. I was obliged to accept it. He would mark my visits on the calendar. Twelve days, still twelve days to go until December 17th.

A week passed, cheerlessly. I looked toward that December 17th as I had towards the date when I was to be discharged. The wait became longer and longer. The afternoons were endless. Three o'clock. Four o'clock. How hard it was to abide these far away dates! How right I had been to keep clear of them to the extent it had been in my power to do so! Could not the many mistakes I had committed be ascribed, in part, to the impatience they filled me with? Had I not just committed another?

An Englishwoman getting on in years lived in the hotel—or rather, like me, resided there. Of what unhappinesses did she preserve memory, to what employment had she put the some sixty years she seemed to have lived, just who was that uncle mired somewhere in Devonshire, that brother who every year spent a few hours in Paris? I did not try to find out. I suspected that she plucked her facial hairs for, on certain days, she had the bloom of youth. A patina seemed to have been brushed over the neutrality of her clean, spotless clothes. I often ran into her in the hotel office where she liked to linger about, for however simple and familiar her behavior, she was unfailingly treated with respect. In spite of the interest I showed in the hotel's remodeling, her presence would relegate me to the background. And, I may add, I would remain there for quite some time, for the owner, while under her spell, didn't think to restore to me my former importance.

One fine day this woman took a sudden shine to me. I must have made some remark that remained with her. Unless the attentions she was the object of had encouraged her to show her true colors. From there on, every time she came upon me she would stop me and oblige me to follow her into the office. But this friendship remained circumscribed. We were friends inside the hotel, but once outside, we unhesitatingly went our separate ways. This could not last. Our relations had become too cordial for me—a Parisian, after all—not to propose to this foreigner that we take some sort of outing together. I stalled as long as I was able. I was all in favor of the relations you establish in the course of everyday life, provided they did not go beyond simple fellowship. This was no longer the case.

One afternoon I was so despondent that the bother of taking this woman out somewhere appeared to me a diversion. We were sitting in the celebrated office one partition wall of which was due to be removed. Outside, the weather was freezing cold. I had my eyes on the door at the far end of the vestibule, looking through its glass at the passers-by, in the constant hope that one might step into the hotel.

"Would you like to go out together?" I suggested all of a sudden.

"And where might we go?" she asked with such a look of gladness that I gazed at her with surprise.

"How about going to a film, for instance?"

"Do you know of one worth seeing?"

"No. We'd be going to the movies just as something to do. That's all."

A half-hour later we were sitting side by side in a little cinema on rue des Ecoles. I was not watching the movie. I was thinking of the six days I had still to wait before seeing Richard. But was this a male delusion?—it seemed to me that my neighbor preferred to lean in my direction whenever the person sitting in front of her obstructed her view of the screen. A glimmer of interest crept into the afternoon. But still, how little desirable this fine woman was! She was talking to herself. I thought of the empty evening ahead of me, of the day that was to follow, of the one after that. My neighbor leaned toward me once again. She started laughing. Then it occurred to me that this woman might be one of those defenseless beings who refuse nothing. Wrinkled and grey-haired though she was, I had an objective. She was still laughing. Anyhow, time was passing more quickly. But what if I was wrong, what if she was really laughing instead of laughing nervously? I brought out a suggestive remark. She continued to laugh. Was I going to place my hand on hers, despite my distaste? For a few moments I wondered about this. I reached out my hand. My neighbor abruptly recoiled. Unbelievable. It was I who aroused distaste in her!

"What's wrong with you?" she asked me curtly.

Then, without another word, she got up and left.

I had not reached the end of my troubles. On the 14th of December I received another letter from Richard. He postponed our get-together until Monday the 24th. He might as well have said that he did not want to see me anymore. After this the Christmas and New Year's holidays would serve as new pretexts. I believed a well thought out plan could be discerned behind all these cancellations. Richard's aim was that on my own I abandon the idea of seeing him. Anger contorted my face. It is a dreadful thing to discover one day that you are at somebody's mercy. Was there a single blunder I had not committed in order to wind up there? I felt I had no one to blame but myself, and this only increased my anger. I had to do something to find relief. Only the wretched telephone lay to hand. I dialed the Europe exchange. But instead of asking for Richard, as I had done the last time, without even inquiring whether he was in I simply left a message that I would be coming on the 17th, that I had nothing else scheduled for then.

The next day I went to Châtillon. A man of my sort doesn't reach the middle of his life without dragging his victims along with him. A man of my sort is weak. My victims! So am I an executioner? I had suffered. I was suffering. Today I continue to suffer. However, the harm I have done has always been reparable, while that which has been done to me . . . I have not asked anything unusual from life. I have asked but one thing. It has always been refused me. I have struggled to obtain it, truly struggled. This thing is something my fellow-creatures get without having to seek it. It is neither money, nor friendship, nor glory. It is a place among men, a place of my own, a place they would acknowledge as mine without envying it, because there wouldn't be anything enviable about it. It would not be distinguishable from their own. It would be respectable, that and nothing more.

I was on my way to see a woman I had once loved, or rather whom I had known intimately. I had not been any more able to end things definitively with Germaine than with Berthe, so that our old, our very old connection still retained a semblance of life. Seventeen years had gone by since I had left Germaine. She had heaped insults and curses upon me. And I had gone back to see her. I wanted at the same time to be free and forgiven. She imagined that I was weak. Maybe I was, after all. Then she believed she was destined to play the heroine's role. Without deviating from her hard-heartedness, she suddenly pretended to feel sorry for me. She allowed me to drop by from time to time. The memory just now came to me of one appalling afternoon when she had invited friends over to meet me. How strange I had found the kindness everyone had displayed!

So I was going out to Châtillon. Oh, the comfort a little trip affords! I took the tram at porte d'Orléans. The weather was cold. The sky was blue. The usual cheerlessness of the flower sellers at the Vanves cemetery was no longer there. You could see into the leafless gardens, and you discovered the hidden benches. I felt happy. The tram seemed possessed of a freedom upon its pre-set course, and I did not have the feeling, as in Paris, that it took too long to get moving again. I was no longer attached to the handful of streets making up a neighborhood. Into my head popped the silly idea of returning in a little while on some one or other of the outer-circle main lines, by way of Saint-Cloud, or the Gare du Nord. Ah, how sweet it would be to set off without money, without purpose and head for our undoing instead of continuing to live in degradation!

In Châtillon I downed two glasses of wine at some refreshment bar opposite the railway station. I wasn't inclined to turn up before noon. It seemed to me that the sky was clouding over, sparkling though the day was. I sensed that I must wait until I was on my way back in order to rediscover the delights I had felt on the way here.

I had not come to Châtillon without a purpose. From five o'clock in the morning when I woke up (as I frequently did when I had trouble falling asleep the previous night) to the time I actually got out of bed, Richard had been on my mind. Then I had an odd idea. Why couldn't I ask Germaine's son to write a letter requesting on his own account what his mother had been for so long after me to do for him? I would show Richard the piece of paper. But, actually, would I? When you got down to it, did I not despise these miserable tricks? I was a man, wasn't I, notwithstanding my shabby behavior? After all, did it matter to me what Richard might decide to do?

Germaine was not expecting me. I caught her looking a sight. This wasn't the first time. In the beginning I had marvelled when she hadn't slipped off on one excuse or another in order to get into some different clothes and fix up her face. I did not suspect that she derived a strange satisfaction from appearing thus to her disadvantage. Then it came to me that this was her way of making me understand that she had ceased to feel anything for me at all.

She greeted me cordially. I should say that however great her animosity against me, she always counted, whenever I visited, upon some indefinable reversal of the situation, some unforeseen gift. So aware of this had I become that instinctively, once inside the door, the first words I spoke were to announce that there was nothing new. She would conceal her disappointment behind the extra work I was the occasion of. She opened cupboard doors, asked me to move aside. I was, instantly, mixed up in all her domestic occupations, without the slightest consideration, without her showing the slightest embarrassment, as if it would have been the height of absurdity to shield me from any everyday unseemliness after what I had done.

Just as we sat down at table, her son appeared. He was a tall young man wearing knickerbockers and a short leather jacket with a zipper. His simplicity and his healthiness were such a pleasant surprise! He was *wholesome*, to use a word his mother was fond of. He was planning to enter an agricultural school. Not for one moment did it puzzle him that I was neither his father, nor his brother, nor his uncle, nor his cousin.

Germaine touched his tie. His sturdy neck sat on broad shoulders. His mother glanced at me. She seemed to be telling me that her son would be able to defend her if need be. For meanness this unspoken allusion to her son's physical strength outdid even the poverties so complacently displayed before me.

I had taken off my overcoat, with reluctance. Wouldn't it have been more sensible, in such a house, to take off nothing at all, to keep standing, to retain one's freedom of movement? In a café did I not always pay as soon as the drinks came so as not to have to wait, so as not to be detained? Lunch lived up to what preceded. Germaine set the pots and pans on the table, asked me to pass them afterward.

What had I come looking for here? A letter I could avail myself of? No.

I felt uncomfortable calling upon Richard before the date he had specified. Anger had led to my decision. I had now regained my self-control.

I rang the bell without hesitation. No valid reason stood in the way of paying him this visit.

The maid left me in the vestibule. Would Richard see me? I could hear the sounds of doors opening and closing, of comings and goings. I had thought that never again would I act on an impulse. Yet was it not an impulse that had brought me here? Suddenly I felt several distinct rivulets of sweat under my armpits. It had just become apparent to me that something had happened in order that I be there, that, as I had believed deep down, my fears were not exaggerated.

A few minutes later, the maid reappeared. She bade me follow her. She led me into a salon. Richard was there waiting for me. As soon as he perceived me, he strode toward me.

"How is it that you are here today?"

"You mean you weren't expecting me?"

By feigning surprise I was hoping to side-track him. Naive exclamations of this sort had enabled me to go over well with many people. I used to think they were deliberate. But they weren't, for though they work to my detriment nowadays, they still keep emerging from my mouth.

"I didn't let you know, that's true, but it's been such a long time since we've seen each other!"

"You think so, do you?"

"Yes."

"Has the time seemed long? You couldn't get on without me any longer?"

"Yes."

"And you arrive at noon, for lunch. Very well then, you'll have lunch with us. It will be charming."

He left the room.

"I've let my wife know. She's most delighted to see you," he told me when a little later he came back to get me.

We had been sitting at the table for ten minutes or so when all at once Richard got up and left the room.

"Don't take offence," his wife said, "Richard is very on edge at the moment."

"What's wrong?"

"Nothing. You must take my word that nothing's wrong."

But on seeing him return I became frightened. There was an unsettled intensity in the gaze he fixed upon me. Instead of quieting him, absence had worsened the state he was in. So it had not been to hide it from me that he had left the room. This simple fact alarmed me. For a moment he remained motionless, his hands on the back of his chair, and then, instead of sitting down, he walked around the table and halted half a pace away from me.

"Miserable. You are a miserable wretch," he said, advancing his head until there was no space between us.

I did not flinch. His wife had leapt up. She seized him by the arm and drew him back to his seat.

"Don't take offence," she repeated.

My lips had remained parted. I had not moved a muscle. I sensed that so long as I maintained my cataleptic rigidity, I was excused from responding, presumably still stunned by the insult. But it was soon clear to me that I couldn't hold this pose indefinitely. I ought to react. What should I do? Unable to come up with some word, some gesture, I started trembling. Finally I cried: "No, no, no . . . I won't accept this . . . It's outrageous. You must apologize. I demand an apology."

Now it was Richard's turn to become immobile. He looked at me without seeming to understand the reason for my agitation. No regret could be made out in his face. Yet, from certain prolonged lowerings of his eyelids, I sensed he was gradually regaining his composure. His clenched hands opened as though in response to heat.

"Do you feel better?" his wife asked him.

He bowed his head several times.

"You must rest yourself."

After having had him sit down she then wanted to make him get up.

"Let me be. I'm not through."

Once more he fastened his strange gaze upon me, then, this time without anger, he repeated: "You're a miserable person."

I turned toward Madame Dechatellux. Through a signal she conveyed to me that I must above all not lose my temper. I replied with another signal that meant that what she was asking was beyond my powers. Then, as if, despite everything, I desired to obey her, I held my tongue.

Richard had turned back into a human being.

"It's over with, isn't it?" his wife asked.

"Yes."

"What possessed you?"

"I don't know."

She was so overwhelmingly solicitous that it seemed this insult had more consequences for him than for me. I stood up.

"Sit down."

"What's this? You're asking me to stay?"

"Please accept my apology. I don't understand what got into me. You know perfectly well I cannot really think the things I said. It would be incomprehensible after all the tokens of affection I've given you. Isn't that so, Edith?"

"You haven't been in top form lately."

"Indeed, I haven't been feeling well these past few days. All of a sudden, I had this need to tell you that you were a miserable person. I would have said the same to my best friend had he happened to be sitting here. It's perhaps because you came though I had asked you not to come."

A half-hour later I took my leave. He saw me to the door.

"Forget the whole thing. Come back next Monday as I asked you to do in my letter. In any case, you can count on me. Tomorrow, I'll send you the money."

I went back to the hotel. There were roses in the office. I stopped to look at and smell them. "I'm a miserable wretch!" Was it possible? I had rarely been insulted in my lifetime, but on every occasion it had happened, I had drawn from it some salutary lesson. "Maybe I am miserable."

*   *   *

Neither the next day, nor the one after that, nor on any of the following days did the money reach me. When an affair is settled after a scene like the one that had just transpired, the carrying out of what has been agreed to seems merely a question of detail, and it is difficult to lodge a claim. I could not believe that Richard would have had the duplicity to count on this scruple. Were we back again in the business of the previous week?

On December 24th I returned to Richard's. An incessant stir was causing the doors to tremble. I had barely sat down in the waiting room when there was a ringing of the telephone, shortly followed by that of the door bell. Several times the maid entered the room where I was sitting. First, she came to fetch a chair, then, stored high up in a cupboard, some chinaware which Madame Dechatellux probably reserved for company. Next, in the lower part of this same cupboard she put away a bundle sewn up in a piece of canvas. I learned later that inside were old linen sheets intended for a nursing home. For a few minutes the door of a small office adjoining the consultation room stood open. I saw a man, seated, alone, dangling his hat between his parted knees. In the room the overhead light was on even though it was daytime. I had been waiting for ten minutes when a thin, commonly dressed woman was shown in. She was holding a sheet of paper in her hand. Noon struck. She sat down across from me, visibly intimidated. Almost at the same moment, the sounds of voices reached us. I recognized Richard's. He was ushering out a patient. On noticing that the connecting door was ajar, he pushed it shut. Nevertheless, he had time to see me, but on his face there was nothing to indicate that he knew me. The sounds of voices now yielded to an extraordinary murmur. The gravity words take on when all you can hear is their sound! Then the man I had glimpsed sitting with his hat between his knees emerged through the doorway of the small office. I looked at him. Now he was holding his hat in his hand like any visitor. He had a white beard and, like many men of that age (he must have been in his sixties), you sensed about him a rather startling disregard for appearances below the waist—uncreased trousers, cracked shoe-leathers— while the haircut, the face, the detachable collar, the cravat formed a studied ensemble. He took a seat between the newcomer and myself, clucking his tongue, blowing his nose, smoothing down his moustache, without concern for my presence or for the lady's.

Suddenly, the door opened again, and Richard called the old man. He sprang to his feet with an astonishing agility. This time Richard gave me a friendly nod. I thought he was calling me as well. I was preparing to join him, without my neighbor's somewhat obsequious briskness. The idea that Richard had arranged for me and the other man to meet shot through my mind, and I felt a brief joy. But I was mistaken. Richard stopped me with a gesture. Two further patients were shown into the waiting room. They were a relatively young married couple. It was clearly the man who was unwell. I was moved by the care with which the woman had her husband sit down, as well as by the apologetic smile she directed at me, as though she had disturbed me. The man looked cadaverous. His cheeks seemed sucked inward. My eyes remained fastened on this couple. Then I noticed something that moved me even more than the woman's devotion. It was how a person's continual presence places a blindfold over our eyes. This woman did not see the state her husband was really in. She kept repeating to him—and I felt it wasn't in order to reassure him but because she herself was convinced—that he was cured,

that but for the urging of a certain Doctor Bodin or Baud-
houin she would never have brought him to see Dechatellux.

These preliminaries decidedly did not bode well. A quarter of an hour later Madame Dechatellux called me discreetly. To be the cause, amidst all these agitations, of a
supplementary agitation filled me with embarrassment. It
was obvious that in order to receive me Richard's wife had
interrupted her pursuits once she could safely get away for
a moment. However certain overlooked details remained,
and every so often she would absent herself. During these
minutes of waiting I could not help but think about the
contrast that showed between Richard's life and my own.
To devote oneself this way to mankind, to relieve its woes,
to dedicate oneself sincerely and with all one's strength to
such a noble task—this was far greater than to live in idleness. Richard would get up every morning at five. One hour
later he would go to communion. Then he would visit
needy patients, to all and sundry disbursing financial aid,
medical attention, advice. He never sat down to lunch before one-thirty. Then he would continue to see patients.
How comforting it must be to be taken up this way by a
thousand occupations, to never be alone with oneself! And
what joy to know that such a bustling life was not spent in
vain!

When Madame Dechatellux reappeared after one of her
brief absences, I said: "It seems to me that Richard is becoming more and more active."

This, she replied, was nothing. Next month her husband
would be directing a free clinic. She would become his
partner. She wasn't complaining. Nor was Richard. The
more they had to do, the happier they were.

At that moment the man with the white beard, who had
made such a bad impression on me because I had detected

in him that awful trait known as late-blooming ambition,
walked up to us.

"May I come in?"

"Why, certainly, Doctor, do by all means come in."

I stood up. Madame Dechatellux introduced me. After
giving my hand a hearty shake he drew Edith off into a
corner. I went over to a window. It was starting to rain
again, and drops were landing on the dry part of the balcony. An electric train swept swiftly past in the cut leading
to the Gare Saint-Lazare. From this high up it looked like
a toy. And so did the passers-by, and the automobiles, and
the houses in the distance. I turned around. Everything in
here was on a human scale. Madame Dechatellux and the
doctor were now standing in the middle of the room. That
fellow was definitely getting on my nerves. Though he was
going on and on I could tell that he had nothing to say, that
the only purpose of this stream of words, punctuated by
predictable gestures, was to keep Edith there.

Richard joined us at last. Egoistically, he allowed his
self-satisfaction to show. It was legitimate, oh, as legitimate as could be, after such a busy morning. He was smiling, but like a man who despite himself is still thinking
about the work he has just left off. With each passing
minute that smile grew brighter. You don't get rid of men-
tal tension the way you do a patient. Richard needed to be
handled gently, given time to regain his bearings. In a
minute or two he would be himself. Would he then recall
the scene from the other day?

"You'll stay for lunch," he said to the doctor who, after
having hung about for so long, was making as if to go.

The telephone rang. Richard excused himself, disappeared. There he was, yes; there was the man who, in the
middle of a conversation, would recall something he had
forgotten, the man who had to be intercepted in mid-career,

who besought you to wait one little moment, who didn't
return, who after that allotted you much more time than
you had asked for; in short, the man I didn't like.

At a quarter of two we sat down to lunch.

"Who's that place for?" Richard inquired, noticing an
empty chair.

"For Mathilde."

"Is she supposed to come?"

"She announced she was coming. As for being able to tell
you whether she actually will. . ."

Richard saw me, heard me. Every so often we exchanged
a few words. He had even very kindly paid me a compli-
ment. But for him I was still one of those innumerable
living beings he had encountered in the course of the morning. I was an element in his entourage. He had not yet had
the time to distinguish me. Suddenly, he clapped his eyes
on me. I felt that little by little he was remembering me,
remembering my last visit, the promise he had made me,
his failure to keep it. No change came about in his attitude.
But when he addressed himself to his wife and to his guest,
from the sound of his voice I could tell that in his view I
had ceased to be some harmless visitor.

The man with the white beard having left, Richard asked
me to come with him. I waited a few moments while he
accompanied Edith back to her room. An accident had be-
fallen her when she was young and she walked with difficulty, using a cane.

"I'll lead the way," he said, passing ahead of me.

Now that he was by himself he exuded a rather disturbing gravity. He opened one door, then another. We reached
his office.

"I'm pleased you came, because I have a good many
things to say to you."

He checked to see that the window was well shut, did much striding about the room in manner of preamble. I had remained standing. I followed him with my eyes. He had the stern expression of men who, before receiving a new visitor, concentrate for a few moments in order rid their minds of the preceding one. After casting a glance at some papers, as if he was not about to lose sight of his overriding preoccupations, he sat down.

"Have a seat," he said to me.

He rose halfway in order to pull up the armchair I had chosen.

"Here we are face to face. I'm delighted. For that matter I knew you'd be coming today. I arranged things so as to be free for the whole afternoon. I hope that you're free as well, Jean."

"Yes."

He appeared satisfied with my answer even though, certainly, he could not have thought for one instant that I might not be free.

"Listen to me, Jean. I'm not going to do what some others would in my place, hemming and hawing and toning down what I have to tell you. I'm going to speak to you frankly. I think that's always the best way to proceed. I didn't send you the money. It wasn't through forgetfulness, it wasn't for economy's sake. I shall not send it to you, in your own best interest. I've thought about it. I have no reason to give you an allowance, absolutely none."

"It's true," I remarked.

Richard's sincerity, as one sees, was contagious.

"Let me finish. I know you're going to ask me a question."

"I shall ask you no question."

"Yes, you will. You are going to ask me why the reasons I have had for supporting you have suddenly disappeared. If

[25]

they were adequate in the past, you ask me, why have they stopped being so today? Here is my answer. I felt sorry for you."

"Sorry! You too!"

"Yes. I warned you I would speak frankly. That is what I am doing. You were misfortunate. . ."

"And today you think I'm not anymore?"

Richard had been on his feet for several minutes. He was pacing the room, hands behind his back. I could not help but find it extraordinary that a man, speaking to me about things that so intensely preoccupied him, could pace back and forth as if he were dictating his correspondence. He planted himself abruptly in front of me: "You've just given yourself away," he exclaimed in triumph. "You've said something that's absolutely characteristic of you. How old are you?"

"Thirty-eight years old."

"I am forty-two. So we're both the same age, more or less, aren't we?"

"Yes."

"And it's one of your contemporaries you blame for not helping you?"

"I don't blame you for anything."

"I am replying to your question. You ask whether I think you're no longer misfortunate. You are misfortunate, you certainly are. I know you continue to be misfortunate. I don't doubt this. But what difference can it make whether you are or aren't? You imagined—you still do—that your misfortunes gave you rights, that they authorized you to demand reparations, compensation. And when I announced to you that I was stopping the handouts, instead of trying to perceive the real motives behind my decision, you immediately think of those misfortunes which, to your mind, should entitle you to so much special treatment. To think that I should forget that you were misfortunate! What hard-heartedness! What insensitivity! What injustice! But even if you were ten times as misfortunate as you are, even if you had to beg in the street, I would act no differently. Four years ago, at a period when I too was unhappy, when the death of my sister. . . You made a gesture—and since I mention it, I'll tell you again that it touched me very deeply and hasn't been forgotten—, you made a gesture which I didn't think you capable of, and which suddenly revealed to me that there was some heart to you. Appearances, my upbringing, all sorts of prejudices had deceived me. Yes, I had been unfair, we all had been unfair. I won't hide it from you, I had regrets. Then I did what you know. And I am not sorry I did. Why have I decided not to give you any more money? Why today instead of yesterday? I am going to tell you. You'll not take it amiss. You made me feel sorry for you. I do not feel sorry for you anymore, not the least bit. For the past four years I have seen the way you live. I thought, as would anyone else in my place, that you were a victim of circumstance, that your misfortunes were owing to the world's unkindness. I did sincerely think so. Today I understand that nobody is responsible for your misfortunes, that they come from you. By assuring your existence I am doing you a disservice, I am preventing you from struggling against your shortcomings. Only a few weeks ago I yet believed you had your heart set on freeing yourself from the tutelage you were living under. How naive! You move into a little hotel in the Latin Quarter, presumably on account of memories attaching you to the area, and you wait. For what? Nobody knows. You wander to left and to right. At the age of thirty-eight, in sound health, you live like an elderly gentleman and when you have an inkling that this existence may cease, you lose your head. Well, it must cease, I am telling you so in your

[27]

own interest, solely in your own interest. Listen to me, Jean, you must have the strength to prefer the direst poverty to such an existence. At least do it for me."

"For you?"

"Yes. I am pained by this situation. It pains me because, for my part, it humiliates me. You are intelligent. You understand me. It's over. I do not want to give you money anymore. I am not going to give you any. I have a family, I have friends. My wife doesn't criticize me. But other people! If I have not hidden from them what I have done for you, I am obliged to hide from them what I know about you. They have suspicions. They wonder what there can be between us. It's perfectly understandable."

The door opened. I glimpsed Madame Dechatellux leaning on her cane, frozen like a spy on the stage when the curtain concealing him is drawn aside. I wasn't startled. Every time Edith left the solitude of her room, she would freeze this way for a few seconds in order to remember what living creatures were like.

"Doctor Sellier wishes to speak with you," she said, glancing at us, her husband and myself, as if, since her arrival, everything we might have said to one another already belonged to the past.

Since the two men had never met one another, the newcomer hesitated slightly, not knowing which of us two, Richard or I, was the master of the house. Thanks to this uncertainty I was for an instant or two the beneficiary of an amiability not intended for me. From the subsequent conversation I gathered that Richard's visitor, although unknown to him personally, was a colleague to whom Richard showed the high mark of esteem of referring those patients for whose care he did not wish to undertake the responsibility.

For a good quarter of an hour the two doctors vied with

each other in courtesies. A friendship was forming before my eyes, one so fervently desired by both parties that they had completely forgotten my presence. It was no longer possible for me to take for myself the graciousness that the visitor's indecision had directed toward me at the start. And when they parted I was surprised they did so on in such a friendly manner before a witness to the newness of their relations.

I remained alone for some time while Dechatellux was seeing his friend out. Daylight was already waning on this winter afternoon. I was thinking about the speech I had just heard. It smelled of midnight oil, preparation, multiple drafts. Richard must have written it, learned it by heart, recited it to his wife. And now I had the impression of having read it somewhere, in an Ohnet novel perhaps. *Listen to me, Jean. . . I'm not going to do what some others would in my place. . .You ask me why. . . You ask me whether. . . Here is my answer. . . I am replying to your question. . . you made a certain gesture. . . and since I mention it I'll tell you again. . .* And the whole thing in such a sincere tone, the "I'm obliged to talk to you this way" tone.

No, something had happened. Just as a certain gesture—to employ Richard's expression—had won me his esteem, so a certain other one—which had probably just been revealed to him—was earning me his contempt. The other day he had shouted at me that I was a miserable wretch. The same thought was in his head while making his speech just now. But he's wrong. I'm not a wretch.

Finally, the door opened again, and through it came Monsieur and Madame Dechatellux. She gazed at me with the look of someone who has just been put in the know. I believe that no woman has ever caused me so disagreeable an impression. She exudes an arrogant harshness and yet, once she unclamps her lips, it is to express herself with a mildness in which not the least trace of condescension can be discerned. I sought to help her walk. She must have imagined that I wished to appear to have forgotten what had just transpired between her husband and myself. She pushed me away, the while saying to me in an affectionate way: "Just go over and sit down."

"I'll sit down in a moment. I want to help you."

This time she accepted, but without uttering a word. After Richard and I had settled her in an armchair, she repeated, still with the same mildness: "Jean, obey."

I sat down with a smile.

"You are smiling, Jean. However this is no time for that."

"I can smile," I rejoined, "there is nothing reprehensible in my smiling."

"My husband has had a long talk with you," she went on. "I also am anxious to speak to you. There are certain things that a woman is better able to get across."

I caught a stern expression on her face. You would expect that an invalid who needs a cane to walk would, once seated, take a comfortable position. Not a bit of it. She hadn't even leaned back. One sensed that she was among those women who consider that in our civilized society they have no need to kowtow to men, despite the weakness of their sex.

"Especially when they are as unpleasant for the person saying them as for the one listening," she continued. "You are not unaware that we know Colonel Laîsné. I even think I recall that you met him in Compiègne four years ago at the home of my husband's parents. He came to see us and, without our having questioned him at all— and on this I give you my word—, he spoke about you. What he said left us literally speechless. And well it might, you will agree. You will agree that relations between us, which might conceivably have gone on, have become impossible."

I didn't flinch. Neither my lips, nor my nostrils, nor my eyelids—nowhere was there a quiver to show the effect of emotion. I saw myself in the room I had had on rue Casimir Delavigne, harmless, solitary. I had expected to be there for a month. Four years had gone by. I had done nothing wrong. With no ambition or desire, I had not even had the occasion to cause hurt. And yet life kept raining blows upon me as it had in the past. Only the cadence had slackened. I grew afraid. Of what? I did not know. And what if I were to act like everybody else? What if I proposed a deal? What if, for money, I accepted being a wretch, accepted never again to return to rue de Rome, accepted never to give any further sign of life? It would have been abominable.

Edith went on.

"You will understand that, given the circumstances, there can be no further question either of our giving you money or indeed of seeing you at all."

Night had all but fallen, and as it would have been disagreeable to look into each other's eyes, no one turned on the lights. Richard maintained silence. He sat back in his armchair as if, coming back to his senses but not yet having recovered consciousness altogether, he dared not take it upon himself to move from the position where he had been placed with the intention of providing him relief.

I got up.

"If Colonel Laisné," I said, "is able to remember a private in the company he commanded nineteen years ago (at which time he was only a captain), a soldier whom he spoke to only once from where he was sitting astride his horse, a soldier without means or personal connections, a soldier like all the others, it is because there is a reason. I am going to tell you what that reason is. It isn't as often as they say that a man finds himself in the presence of an injustice. Whenever that happens to him, he doesn't forget it. And he is even likelier not to forget it if the position he holds prohibits him from redressing it."

Upon those words I left Dechatellux and his wife, taking care not to add anything at all for fear of diminishing their impact. The sky was overcast, there was not a break, not a chink in its despairingly uniform grayness. Passers-by marched forward, head up. Everyone's thoughts were exclusively upon his own business, upon his own little world. And I was like the rest. I have so little malevolence in me that I was thinking that Richard and Edith, especially Richard, had after all not fully exploited my weak point. They had acted without taking any notice of it as if I belonged to their milieu. They had ended our relations with propriety. I walked past the buildings. Inside each of them were families, animosities, rivalries, loves. Was I the only person dwelling upon his behavior? The differences that so preoccupy me melted away on contact with the crowd. The latter grew more and more dense as I approached the Gare Saint-Lazare. Don't we all ponder our deeds? What was going to become of me? When the effects of an event will become manifest only later on, when what has occurred is not misfortune itself but rather the preconditions that make it inevitable, you feel a sense of relief. It seems that we are going to take advantage of the freedom our mind has just recovered. We are going to take decisions. Our enemies can do us no further harm. We are already no longer the man they overcame, but someone else. Was I soothed by these reflections? Yes and no. Never before had I experienced such a feeling of impotence. When everything slips away from us, we take thought and ask ourselves to what extent we are responsible for what is befalling us. Had the

hour struck for the paying for my sins? Perhaps our break-
ing off would prove profitable to me. All I possessed in this
world was a roof over my head. But that meant dealing
with the monthly hotel bill, a bill upon which there appeared pots of tea ordered and forgotten about, ten per cent
service charges, and to which were pinned the pages from
a notebook recording what I owed the laundress. Would I
still be in any position to conduct my life?

That evening, as was happening more and more frequently, I could not prevail upon myself to go to bed. The
later it became, the less sleepy I felt. I picked up a book. To
read at a time like this! I started pacing. A realization
struck me. Without being aware of it I had placed myself at
the mercy of a single person. I had chosen not to exercise
foresight. What stupidity! Every so often I stopped, glanced
around. I was the occupant of this tiresome room. I came
back here every time I went out. But what if one day I did
not come back! Let's imagine this. For perhaps a week
nobody would dare touch my bed-sheets, my personal belongings. They wouldn't disturb my things. They would
remember all my physical particularities, and not my in-
solvency. My personality, so vague up until then, would
take on relief. If only it were thus, but with me there!

Until then, the events of my life had all linked themselves together. A host of ties—certain ones of which, ad-
mittedly, were very flimsy—connected me to the past. My
isolation, great as it was, was not comparable to a refugee's.
For instance, I had lost sight of my mother years ago. We
could chance upon one another. A few words would be
enough to make her understand how and why I was living
on rue Casimir Delavigne. But tomorrow, when I would be
forced to leave the hotel, without baggage, without my
overcoat perhaps, what would ensue? I took fresh heart
when I reminded myself that I had had these same thoughts

at all the crucial moments of my existence. Had it not, each and every time, been restored to me—that continuity whose loss so frightened me?

I started pacing the room again. I was as tired as if I had walked miles (perhaps I had), and yet all I needed to do was sit down. To sit down in a bedroom! The one armchair held out its arms to me every time I went past it, but just at the prospect of dropping into it I would feel a dizziness, as if after spinning in a circle I had been brought to an abrupt halt. "What am I to do? What am I to do?" I murmured. I lit a cigarette, my thirtieth. They had an ever more bitter taste, but I went right on smoking. It was three in the morning. On waking up, the tip of my tongue would feel prickly. I was thirsty, but I couldn't abide the water in my room. For one instant I thought of going out. To go down five flights of stairs, create the suspicion that I was escorting some woman home—and what after that? Look for somebody to talk to? A kind of fellowship exists out on the street and in cafés during the final hours of the night. Invite a stranger over to my table? Tell him my life story? Those outpourings now belonged to the past. Nowadays money played too great a role in my existence. The stranger would have asked me to stand him to a drink, and I would have wound up in the position I so dreaded, that of the person who does all the paying. My glance strayed over to my bed. Lie down? Sleep? If I could get some sleep, by tomorrow morning I would be restored to my normal state, which was endurable. I opened the window. So much light from my room was projected upon the building across the way that I switched off the electricity. Rue Casimir Delavigne was deserted. I would have to wait until the next day to see living creatures. In the end I sat down in my armchair, I shut my eyes. My head was reeling. I got up, I started walking again. To clear my path I needed only to move a chair. For hours on end I made a detour around this chair, careful each time not to bump into it. Finally I pushed it out of the way. Oh that gesture! To push a chair out of the way in order to make room for oneself! No, I couldn't stay here any longer. I put on my overcoat and went out.

One morning I discovered snow upon opening the curtains. The snowfall had turned back the clock twenty years. Not a sound in the street though I saw passers-by come and go. Not an automobile. It looked as if everyone had decided to go out on foot. Paris was suddenly a Paris of former times. Snow clung precariously to all the cornices. My room was bright. Oh what a delightful morning I spent getting myself together! All that I usually found so distressing—the unmade bed, belongings strewn about—, in this brightness everything was cheerful. It was as in some tale. By simply touching objects I felt busy. Voices were ringing in the hallway. Everybody was united as if within a family.

Suddenly I heard knocking, what sounded like the three raps of people you don't know. Someone had just undertaken to trudge up the five flights on my account. In this hotel, they had never managed to give any precise shape to the ceremony concerning visits. It depended on the mood of the moment. Either the visitor was given a room number and left to fend for himself, or else he was asked to wait while chambermaids were tracked down by means of telephone calls to various floors.

"Come in."

Much to my surprise I stood face to face with the chambermaid.

"A gentleman is waiting for you downstairs."

"Who is it?"

"I don't know."

"All right, I'll be right there."

I was worried. Never did anyone come looking for me in the morning. A few moments later, in the downstairs hallway, a man walked up to me.

"Are you Monsieur Jean-Marie Thély?"

"That's who I am, yes."

"I would like to have a brief word with you."

He inspected the premises through his pince-nez.

"Is there no place here where we could be by ourselves?"

I asked him whether he couldn't tell me, right away, in three words, what this was all about.

"Couldn't we step into this room?" he asked, indicating the office the English lady had been fond of.

"If you insist."

"I don't especially insist. We would simply be able to talk more comfortably."

Once we were seated, the visitor said to me: "Maître Logelin, whom you know, has instructed me to request that you come by his office. He will be expecting you tomorrow, at four o'clock, unless you're not free, in which case I will be most obliged if you will set a day when you are."

Nine years had gone by since I had last been in contact with Maître Logelin. Our relations came back to my mind. As always, their suspension had been owing to some incorrectness on my part that I could not even remember, the upshot being that had I had subsequent need of his advice I would not have dared show my face in his office, and had our paths crossed I would have pretended not to know him. My memory was of a man who had impressed me with his elegance, his distinction, his straightforwardness. When circumstances brought me to his office almost daily over a ten-day period, he was especially congenial with me. He had asked me a great many questions. He found my situ-

ation amusing. He had of course surmised what was going
on behind the scenes, and if in accordance with the canon
of professional conduct he publicly aligned himself with
fortune and stability, in private with me he did not fail to
criticize the harshness and the meanness of his clients.
"You are deluding yourself," was his response upon my
revealing some secret or other that would certainly make
me blush if I could remember it.

For what reasons did he wish to see me today? I was
hoping, without much believing, that he had suddenly remembered me. Do we not sometimes take advantage of the
time that has elapsed in order to try to discover how a
given situation, whose evolution we may not have been in
a good position to follow, has finally turned out? No. Richard had merely requested his notary to see me. So I was
going to find myself, tomorrow, standing before Maître Logelin. And in what circumstances! I would no longer be the
young man who arouses curiosity, about whom one wonders whether it's just luck that he has or whether he's
clever. Maître Logelin will understand immediately. One
day he told me: "Later on in life, after you have my experience, you'll know that a wise managing of one's fortune
is not incompatible with the wildest audacities of the imagination." And I was now to reappear before him with experience. But what experience!

I went to our appointment. I was not slow to perceive
that time is not kind to that sort of disabused sympathy.
Maître Logelin had put on weight. He greeted me with
polite indifference. Once he had striven to make a glitter-
ing impression on me. Not only did he no longer see the
point of such efforts, he did not even remember them. I was
not alone in having lived during these last years. When
formerly he had spoken about his experience, he did not
suspect there was still more of it in store for him. He must

have suffered. Outward appearances counted less for him. Was this the same man who one day had complimented me upon my taste? No longer did he feel that pleasure in drawing himself up to his full height, in treading the carpet in his new shoes.

"Have a seat," he told me without the least allusion to our past relations.

Perhaps because he did notwithstanding preserve some vague recollection of them he may have been saying to himself: "This is Jean-Marie Thély sitting here in my office. Let's see now. What was this about? Where did I put the doctor's letter? Ah, here's the file. Very good." He picked up the letter between his fingertips with that touch of scorn government officials have for the fanciful formats of private correspondence, then, pressing down on the edge of the desk with both hands, he bent forward. "Let's just see now what this letter says. Rue Casimir Delavigne, that's where you live? In the hotel of the same name?"

"Yes, Maître."

He raised his voice as he sat back in his chair.

"I have received this letter from Monsieur Richard Dechatellux. Here's what Monsieur Richard Dechatellux says."

Maître Logelin read the first lines for himself, under his breath. Then, coming upon a passage concerning me, he re-read it aloud. "My wish," Richard had written, "is for you to make him understand that I bear no animosity toward him" (" 'him' means 'you'," Maître Logelin interjected), "and that I am acting from no motive other than my personal convenience." (Here the lawyer started muttering again. Only after turning the page did he decide that he could resume reading aloud.) "I would like you to tell him that through your office I am having him paid a sum of eighteen thousand francs, representing twelve monthly re-

mittances of fifteen hundred francs. It would be shrewd-
ness on your part to induce him to place this sum in your
care. He might have greater need for it later on than he does
today. It is possible, moreover, that the feeling of owning a
sum set safely aside may awaken in him the desire to in-
crease its size, which, I assure you, would be a good thing
for him.' "

Maître Logelin broke off his reading.

"The rest doesn't concern you. You see, I have hidden
nothing from you. My liking for you has even led me to
commit a slight indelicacy with respect to Monsieur Dechatellux. He might not be overjoyed to find out that I read
to you from his letter."

I sensed that the notary's relations with Richard had
changed, and from this I was profiting in a rather unexpected way, since Maître Logelin's relations with me had
changed too. Although offered a far more substantial mor-
sel than in the past, his curiosity disdained it. At one time
he had given me excellent advice on the management of
my future fortune, and today it did not even occur to him
to ask himself how on earth I was reduced to accepting
charity. No irony in his voice. No display of false pity.
Decidedly, in this year 1938 a truce was in effect in men's
affairs. Failure in life, which for so long had seemed to me
like a sort of dishonor, no longer had the same importance.
Because of the political events that were having their impact upon all of us, we no longer felt ashamed at not having
got anywhere. Never as at this moment had I felt this comforting sensation that comes from the equality of all in the
face of danger.

Without bluster, without provocation, without postur-
ing, in a tone that the least little thing might have caused
to falter, and above all being very careful to forestall any
suspicion that I was refusing with a view to obtaining more,

I responded that I was very touched by Richard's kindness, but that I was not able to accept this money.

"No, that's how it seemed to me," Maître Logelin observed.

It was dark outside when I left the office. Reflections of brightly-lit storefronts shimmered upon the frosted sidewalks, as if in stirring water. I was in that state of excitement where I am put by marks of esteem. It seemed to me that I no longer had anything to blame on anyone. I was imagining to myself that we all shared a consciousness of having been in the wrong, and that we were better people for it.

A few days later I found a bill from the hotel in my pigeonhole, the second notice. The owner emerged from his office at that same moment. By way of excuse, he said: "I thought you had forgotten me."

"No, no, I hadn't forgotten you."

Slowly I climbed the five flights. At present it bore in upon me that I had been a bit too neglectful of reality. Time goes by. You are absorbed. You live without thinking that every least thing is entered in the account. And, all of a sudden, you discover that the month just ended which was nothing but worries is costing as much as if it had consisted of nothing but joys.

It was five o'clock. I stretched out across the bed in such a way that my feet, remaining not far from the floor, prevented me from having that feeling of inertia I would have felt lying full length. My fingers were interlaced behind my neck. I had a headache, and this pressure on my nape soothed the pain. I didn't dare draw on my cigarette from fear the ash would fall.

"What's this! You're lying down!" exclaimed Berthe, who had walked in without knocking.

Out of a wish to heighten the appearance of our intimacy she would take advantage of my disinclination to show any surprise whenever someone popped up in front of me.

"You ought to turn on the lights, close the shutters, get up. What's wrong with you today?"

I conveyed my cigarette, held at a steady angle, to the marble top of the nightstand.

"Nothing's wrong."

"Get up then. We're going out for a walk."

"It's raining."

"What difference does that make? You're coming with me."

"If I come with you, I won't come back. No, no, I'd rather stay here."

Whenever Berthe visited me I would follow her eyes, for she was always trying to detect changes that would allow her to draw unpleasant conclusions. This time I shut my eyes.

"I don't see the matches," she said.

"Why?"

"Since you want to stay, I'm going to make you tea."

"There's no sugar."

"Well then I'll go out and get some. Come along, let's show a little life. Aren't you ashamed to just let yourself go this way?"

It no longer annoyed me to be talked to this way. Its heartiness rang false to me, that was all. Once by myself, I got up, closed the shutters. There were times when it did me good to be submissive. I scrubbed my face with the damp corner of a towel. I shook a little brilliantine on my hair. From the top shelf of the mirrored armoire I took down the spirit lamp, the teapot, the cups. Then I lit another cigarette.

"That's very good. You've done something positive," Berthe told me on her return.

"Haven't I though."

"What's wrong with you?"

"I've already told you nothing's wrong."

"You look drowsy."

"Maybe I am sleepy. The tea will wake me up."

I watched Berthe bustling about. She enjoyed domestic chores when she performed them at other people's places, at mine, for instance. Why at my place? Was I capable of appreciating her homemaker's skills? For a second I almost told her to leave. I raised a hand above my head, then let it fall lifelessly, as though it no longer belonged to me.

"Where are the little teaspoons?"

"I don't know. I don't have any little teaspoons."

Berthe looked hard at me without saying a word.

"I've had enough," I said.

"You've had enough of what?"

"I've had enough. That's all."

"Listen to me, Jean. There's nothing more tiresome than innuendos."

"What innuendos? I'm happy, honestly happy."

I raised my hand again, fingers closed, but this time to the height of my face, then I opened my hand. This gesture symbolized a blossoming.

"In that case," Berthe said, "I can say just one thing to you: everything is perfect."

"I'm the happiest man on earth."

"I'm very glad. Very glad. You won't hear me begrudging you. Where's the tea?"

"In the armoire."

"If you keep this up, Jean, I'm going."

"No, no, stay. I repeat that I'm happy. Maybe it's because you're here."

Berthe turned away from me. I walked up to her on tip-toe, doing a parody of a "lover surprising his fiancée." At one point the thought of grabbing her by the shoulders, with apparent tenderness, entered my mind. But I restrained myself. There was something about this charade that shocked me.

We had tea. I calmed down. Berthe took advantage of this to tell me she understood neither why I didn't ask Richard to find me a position, nor how I could live like this without a job. "I'm still very fond of you. That's why I'm taking the liberty of telling you this."

Finally, she left me to myself.

I ceased to think about Richard. You would have imagined he had never existed. The series of events that had unfolded over the past four years had completely vanished from my memory. Even at night, when I was alone in my room, no recollections arose in my mind. I would step out, I would say a few words to this person and to that person, chat in restaurants, all that without anything ever reminding me of Richard's existence. Nevertheless, I sensed that this forgetting would not last. Was it the effect of weariness, was it a reaction to having focussed for too long on the same subject? It gave me no peace. When I least expected it I noticed I had trouble breathing. Then there appeared the feeling of something like cowardice. In order to take my mind off Richard I had to not think about the future, to refrain from introducing the slightest changes into my habits.

So long as the sky remained gray I remained in this nebulous state. But one morning in early February sunshine poured into my room. There wasn't a cloud left. It was mild outside. I opened the window and breathed in deep lungfuls. I was coming back to life and, for the first time in three weeks, I was reminded of Richard. Then I understood what had taken place inside me. I understood that there was a course of action I ought to have taken, and that by keeping Richard at a remove from my thoughts I had spared myself from taking it. I understood that I had lacked strength. That course of action consisted not in disappearing mysteriously, in such wise that there be no knowing whether I was desperate or furious, but to the contrary in clearly proclaiming my resolve. In letting my relations with the Dechatellux family conclude in a scene so little to my advantage as had been the one at rue de Rome, I seemed to wish to put myself in a humiliating posture in order to render Richard's harshness more striking. In this way I would still have hold of him. Therein lay my cowardice. But was I going to have the courage—I who had however demonstrated this courage in my actions—to say or write to Richard that as of today our relations were *definitively* severed?

One evening, as I was coming in, the owner asked me to accompany him into his office.

"You don't look," he said to me, "as if you realize the situation you're in."

"Oh, but I do, I do, I realize it perfectly."

"One wouldn't think so. You're not doing anything. I see you pass by every day without even showing so much as a trace of embarrassment. I'd say that takes a fair amount of cheek."

"What do you want me to do?"

"It isn't for me to tell you."

"You know very well that I will pay you."

"That's precisely what I wonder about."

"Any day now."

I went up to my room. " 'Any day now.' Why did I say that?" I muttered. I was tempted to go back down to confess to the owner that nobody would ever again be giving me any money. But I decided to wait until the next day.

"What do you intend to do if I do not pay my bill?" I asked the owner, drawing him aside.

He gazed at me, dumbfounded. He did not understand my question.

"What do you mean?"

When I put my question to him a second time, his immediate impulse was to declare that he would throw me out. But he feared a trap.

"I think there's a misunderstanding," he said.

"There is no misunderstanding."

"Yes, there is. Since you've been here, you've always been on time. There's something behind your question. I'll tell you what. If you're having money troubles, just say so. I'd prefer knowing."

"I'm not having any troubles. I shall pay you. And if I don't, you will do whatever you like."

These conversations were being repeated more and more often. I then noted a very strange phenomenon. My fatalism inspired confidence in the hotel owner and even aroused in him the hope of heaven only knows what future windfall.

One evening I received a *pneu* from Edith. She directed me to call at her parents' home the next day at four o'clock. The comminatory tone clearly showed that to her mind she was doing me an honor. What did she have to tell me? Was the time nigh when my life was to be filled with tedious questings? I had to run, at four o'clock in the afternoon, to a far corner of Auteuil. And, of course, it was raining. Trembling reflections, sprouting from the sky like mistletoe, disappeared into the asphalt. Up until this point my actions had proceeded from a series of reasonings. The result had hardly been encouraging. Now I had decided to follow my impulses.

At present I felt, without knowing why, as if I were a sort of creditor. The punishment was beginning. To get rid of me I would be sent off to one address after another. I would have to wait everywhere. I would be treated like a tradesman who pads his bills. Shouldn't I have written to Richard that I fully understood his attitude, thanked him for having wished to have a relatively large sum turned over to me, not given him the impression that I was withdrawing into my shell, always a sign of weakness? It was too late. In Auteuil I was going to hear dead things talked about by a woman who thought they were alive. Well, all I'll have to do is keep still, maintain a good respectful silence.

Mirrors cast back reflections of me and when a door opened I saw myself being whisked away and then back to where I stood. I walked up to the mezzanine. No need to summon the elevator into action. I climbed the shallow, carpeted stairs without needing to shorten my stride. What was I doing in such a setting, with all that height above me? I leaned on the thick polished banister to catch my breath, or at least I thought that was the reason.

An elderly lady was sitting near a marble fireplace where some logs were burning. Edith introduced me, invited me to sit down.

"I asked you to come to my mother's," she said, "because I was anxious to have a conversation with you without my husband present. I have the feeling that, without him there, it will be easier for us to reach an understanding."

But an understanding about what, for God's sake?

MY LIFE

What is one to make of the following story?

After two hours of battling tooth and nail, the daughter of a poor woodcutter gives up the struggle. The scene takes place in the garden of an old house belonging to a charitable lady in Compiègne. There is a lowering sky. Spring has just begun. The still leafless branches have the suppleness of switches. Now and then the man has paused for a little rest, showing no shame at thus seeming to be harnessed to a lengthy undertaking. Yet he is neither a soldier, nor a laborer, nor a domestic, nor a tradesman. He is an officer in the dragoons, Second Lieutenant Le Claud.

He is a fine sort of fellow, not very intelligent, who received a good education from the Christian brethren. He knows that he has just willfully transgressed religious law. He could not live in a state of sin. At mess he is not in his usual gay spirits. He is preoccupied. He notices the fact, and not without a little glow of pride. It is not given to every man to have a moral life, is it? That evening he sees his victim again. She is charming in her confusion. He desires her yet more ardently than he did the first time. But he will respect her.

Nine months later, a child is about to be born on the small estate at Cuts where Madame Mobecourt has sent her protégé. The caretakers convey the news. The old lady hastens to Cuts, even though night has fallen. There is frost. She contemplates the stars inserted at varying depths within the sky, the watery whiteness of the moon above a frozen landscape. On arriving, she makes out lights in the central part of the manor. She thinks: "The caretakers have taken it upon themselves to open the house. They did well." The child? He is red enough to explode. He really does not correspond at all to the tiny, defenseless creature Madame Mobecourt had been expecting to find. He waves his fists. He shrieks. When he stops, you are eager to believe he has calmed down. But all he is doing is catching his breath.

I am that child.

There exist people who are convinced that it is how you start out that counts most in life. If it is a bad start we get, the worst misfortunes may well befall us. By this they are not disturbed. For it was inevitable. But if our start is a good one and the worst misfortunes befall us anyway, the same people are sincerely distressed. And so, when the moment has come to register the infant's birth, Madame Mobecourt exerts her authority to defer the establishing of the certificate, so as to permit the father to make himself known. Monsieur Nicaise, recently arrived from a third-rank subprefecture, takes no little pride in giving the departmental seat an idea of the tact to be deployed in his district. And the response to Madame Mobecourt is couched in customary and kindly-disposed administrative reserve: "To oblige you, Madame, we shall wait, but we entreat you not to delay too long." This detail has its importance for, nineteen years later, it was accountable for the child's inclusion in the 1919 draft rather than in that of 1918.

A few days later, Madame Mobecourt, who has succeeded in getting the young mother to talk, requests a visit from Second Lieutenant Le Claud. There then ensues the strangest of conversations. The officer accepts no blame. He does not acknowledge the right of anyone to meddle in his moral life. He will not tolerate anyone likening him to an everyday seducer, still less so to a satyr. "One must not forget after all that Mademoiselle Marguerite was compliant." Furthermore, he has a clear conscience. He knows what he did afterward. Madame Mobecourt utters an exclamation of surprise. Why yes, absolutely, he did his duty. If he does not wish to say in what way, it is out of respect for his interlocutor. There are subjects that he is unable to broach with a lady. What would her opinion of him be if he spoke to her about masculine desire? "Only a man can understand me," he says by way of conclusion.

Accordingly my grandfather, François Thély (derived from *theil: tilleul*, linden tree, in *langue d'oïl*) was a woodcutter. He exaggerated his misfortunes, which was altogether needless. A widower with eight children, alcoholic, his right side paralyzed following a stroke, I picture him living in a rustic but nonethclesss squalid hut in the middle of the Laigle forest. He was, it seems, a draft dodger, an anarchist, without even the instinct to pull off the tatters hanging from his clothes. He refused all help from others, thereby, he fancied, instilling in them some sort of guilt. Everyone had grown tired of him. The officials and staff at the various charitable organizations in the region had finally foisted him off on Madame Mobecourt, not without proposing among themselves to observe in what manner she would handle the situation.

How strangely the word grandfather rings to the ear of a man who never knew his parents! And the nicely balanced sentence which follows: "I am the son of an officer who seduced a poor girl taken in by a charitable lady"—does it

not, it too, ring strangely to my ear? I am the son of an
officer who seduced a poor girl. . . "Officer," "seduced,"
"poor girl"—all they are is words, like "grandfather."

They say that after giving birth to me, my mother remained
in Cuts for two years. She must have done chores at the
farm. The place had nothing pastoral about it. Heavens no.
One hundred seventy acres of beet fields. My mother loved
me, I have been told, as only misfortunate young mothers
can. Then, one day, she disappeared. They didn't know
whether she had left, whether she had dropped dead in the
middle of the woods, whether she had drowned herself in
the Aisne. Madame Mobecourt had a sister in Versailles
who, by happy coincidence, adored children. I was taken
there. What happened then? I don't know. In any event I
was brought back to Cuts a few years later. But while the
gatekeepers still occupied the lodge at the entrance to the
estate, the latter no longer belonged to Madame Mobecourt. The elderly lady had for a long time hesitated to sell
it, uncomfortable at the idea of abandoning all the humble
folk who gravitated around her. But in all likelihood she
was eventually obliged to do so.

The buyer, a Parisian by the name of Rigal, succeeded
her. He had the usual features of a newcomer. He was
attentive lest he commit a mistake. From fear of doing the
wrong thing, he was equally polite with everyone.

I imagine him being taken about the estate. Monsieur
Rigal looks with interest at what he is being shown, but his
mind is far away. What interests him is invisible. It is the
position he will occupy in the region. Passing the gatekeepers' lodge, Madame Mobecourt advises him to retain these
excellent servants.

On his second visit she returns to the question of the
gatekeepers, then, for the first time, she talks about the

abandoned little boy—me—whom they look after with such devotion. Later on, she will tell my story, ask the buyer to allow the gatekeepers to keep me under their roof.

Actually Monsieur Rigal enjoyed playing a role in the countryside. He saw himself intervening in disputes, maintaining some privileges, doing away with some abusive ones, granting still others. He informed himself carefully regarding local customs. Already a property owner in Paris, he tried to cut the figure of a man of experience. But that was not the same thing. He was forever discovering new prerogatives which filled him with secret joy. He agreed to buy.

The deeds signed, he will not concern himself about the extent to which my insignificant person is in his charge.

Freed of the worry of running this estate, Madame Mobecourt will not be concerned about it either.

As for the gatekeepers, their belief is that, for the time being, others are grateful to them for raising me.

One day my mother reappeared. There was that kind of decorousness about her bearing and dress that one finds in people who have risen from poverty. Her clothes, her hat, her gloves, her stockings, her boots, her handbag made one think they had been bought with honest money. What had she done during those years? I shall not talk about that. I shall say simply that a guardian angel must have been watching over her, since she had come out of those obscure years with her health intact, and because a vice squad inspector had released her one night, not out of pity, but out of momentary disgust for the profession he exercized.

So then, my mother had come back. She was only twenty-seven years old. She was convinced that hard times would never return. She appeared not to remember her relationship with Madame Mobecourt. The latter was somewhat shocked by this. Did it not thus seem that my mother meant to place herself on an equal footing with her benefactress? She charged no one with responsibility for her misfortunes. In return, she asked that in her regard others give proof of the same generous attitude.

She came, she kissed me, and that very same evening, she left again. Why this lone and brief visit in the middle of my childhood?

A year later, Monsieur Rigal was forced to leave Cuts for a reason unknown to me. He was regretted by no one, although with time he had made himself attractive and had begun to be liked.

After him a certain Monsieur Vialatte bought the estate.

My memories grow sharper. I am eleven years old. I am still living with the gatekeepers. They had not lost their jobs despite all the changes. But they had lost most of the virtues that had made them faithful and loyal servants. They did not hide the fact that I was an encumbrance (in Cuts!), that what Madame Mobecourt paid them for my keep was insufficient to feed me. And, too, they had children of their own. They did not complain openly, however. They were afraid that I would be placed with relatives or friends, and end up better off than their own children here.

Monsieur Vialatte's daughter, Jacqueline, took six months to distinguish me from the other children. This was my first discovery of how difficult it is in life to get the obvious acknowledged. In any case, she took particular notice of me. I must say that I did my utmost to attract her attention, to make her understand that I had nothing in common with the gatekeepers' children. Be that as it may, she did not speak to me. From fear of having to make a choice, she preferred leaving things such as they were. I remember that the gatekeepers would pat me on the head while she was there, but that, once we were out of her sight, they would slap me about. Then she avoided passing by the gatehouse. She probably suspected what was going on behind her back, but as she couldn't do anything to prevent it, and as she may have liked me a little, she refrained from going out by the main gateway.

From that moment on I beheld the gatekeepers as my enemies. Whatever brutalizing my pretension earned me, I refused to follow the other children towards their fate. Whenever I caught sight of Mademoiselle Vialatte in the distance, I tried to catch her attention. I would provoke thrashings. I sensed that especially cruel treatment could alone rescue me from my wretched condition. But the moment any person apt to report what he had seen would appear on the horizon, kindnesses were substituted for backs of the hand. It was doubtless during this period that I developed the shameful fault of feeling myself diminished by the presence at my side of anybody of a quality inferior or even equal to mine.

Impossible to get myself mistreated before witnesses? One day, however, I had the luck of receiving a blow with a stick at the very moment Jacqueline, returning from Compiègne, rolled up in her "break". I let myself sink to the ground, howling.

Abel Moreux' profession was that of a real estate agent. He had no children. He knew everything that went on in and around about Compiègne. Hence he knew of my existence. Spending your life as an intermediary in other people's dealings does not mean that you are satisfied with such a minor role. Along with everyone else, you have secret ambitions. Though you pretend to be content with a simple percentage, you keep your eyes peeled nonetheless. And when a genuine bargain comes along, it's natural that you earmark it for yourself.

Had word of the blow with the stick got around? I don't recall. The fact remains that Abel suddenly appeared at that juncture. He called on Madame Mobecourt. In the end it was generally agreed that I be entrusted to this man. Conditions were imposed upon him, however. He had to do for me what no one had dreamt of doing, he had to agree to put me in a private school, had to treat me like a son.

I experienced one of the greatest joys of my life when, these negotiations completed, Jacqueline refused to let me leave Cuts. Madame Mobecourt backed out of the agreement without the slightest compunction. She liked to appear fickle with businessmen.

I was persuaded that the next day I would say goodbye to my tormentors. But after two months had passed without my life changing in the least, I went back to provoking beatings. To my great surprise, the gatekeepers betook themselves to Monsieur Vialatte with the announcement that they couldn't look after me anymore. For an instant I was seized by panic. I had just learned that to know what we want is not easy.

A mile away lies another estate which, unlike Monsieur Vialatte's, is not in a languishing condition. It belongs to Jules Dechatellux. In the neighboring village they still talk about the considerable sums he spent making the house livable and transforming the inextricable tangle that surrounded it into a charming French garden. It should be added that the species of respect such expenditures inspired in the neighboring landowners had vanished when, over the course of years, they perceived that all this derived less from a desire to live luxuriously than from some sort of craze.

Perhaps I become a little too animated when talking about estates. It's that they have occupied a large place in my life. They influenced my childhood. Like those unsuccessful lawsuits which for certain people are reminders of some sort of past splendor, these estates for a long while gave me the illusion of origins of which I could be proud.

Monsieur Jules Dechatellux was the sort of whom people used to say (they do not say it anymore nowadays): "Ah, what a modest man!" They forgave him his coldness. Monsieur Vialatte alone disliked him. Whenever he met Jules Dechatellux it was to be made conscious that he possessed the smaller fortune, and to feel himself somehow a child. He felt without authority, without weight. This hostility provided me an ill-defined delight. In my imagination the two men were equally powerful. And whenever Monsieur Vialatte went over to visit the wealthy sugar producer, I would watch for his return, for I had noticed that he would treat me then with great gentleness.

One autumn afternoon, Jacqueline took me for an outing in the forest. To invite someone to come on an outing, is that not a great mark of friendliness? The rays of sunshine blended with the forest colors. I remember how I had come running when Jacqueline called me, how when a few steps away I had come to a halt, docile and respectful.

Jacqueline was accompanied by Etienne, a son of Monsieur Dechatellux. I see him now. He had an odd, waddling gait. In any sport you need long training in order to execute certain movements. When you have not had such training, you cannot, simply through imitation, execute those movements. Well, Etienne seemed not to have been trained in life's simplest movements.

It was time to go back. Feelings of regret at bringing a child back to where we had got him at a time when we are continuing to do things that cause him such joy—I sensed those feelings in Jacqueline, and they consoled me. She was a woman who was tortured by the suffering of children. I now understand why she was so slow to commiserate with me. She knew that if she allowed me to place some hope in her, she would not have the courage to rebuff me.

A few days after this outing, Monsieur Vialatte installed me in Sceaux, in the home of one of his friends, a professor at Lakanal. Jacqueline took me to the train. She opened the door to a compartment. She had only to bid me to step up inside for me to obey. Had she changed her mind, had she told me to get off, I would have climbed back down. That omnipotence affects me to this day.

Jacqueline married shortly afterward. She was twenty-eight. To wait for a man who is worthy of one's love—that is a fine thing, especially when it is not a wait that will go on for a whole lifetime, but a reasonable kind of wait.

As a youngster Etienne had been one of those who are continually prey to severe illnesses. He had never finished school. When he had revealed his love for Jacqueline, his father had shown great surprise. For miles around there was no other girl from a middle-class household. That she somehow possess all the virtues, all the qualities making her worthy to become his daughter-in-law, this would indeed have been a most curious coincidence. You did not have to be a great psychologist to understand that this was a love born from circumstances and not from a true community of feelings and of interests. Monsieur Dechatellux opposed this marriage.

It was celebrated all the same, Etienne's state of health preventing his father from maintaining his refusal for very long. Immediately afterward, they left Cuts. I was thirteen at the time. I shall always remember the distress which invaded me when, on returning from Sceaux, I found that Jacqueline was no longer there. I was learning that absence is always fraught with danger.

Yet I had been away for hardly any time at all. I should say that, above all else eager to have me off his hands, Monsieur Vialatte, who was not a very scrupulous man, had not given his professor friend a clear account of my situation. He must have thought that once I was gone, he would find a way not to have to take me back. After all, I did have a mother who might invoke her rights. Madame Mobecourt had never officially ended her involvement in my care. Once I was no longer on the premises, Monsieur Vialatte did not see what made his obligations toward me greater than, for example, Monsieur Rigal's. The professor had questioned me at length. More familiar than his friend Vialatte with the problems brought on for their guardians by the improbable situation certain children are in, he had been prompt to have me sent for on some excuse or other. In his reply Monsieur Vialatte begged the question, pretending not to have understood what was asked of him, in order to buy time. The professor dispatched a registered letter to him by return mail. That was how, having gone off for an indefinite period, I was back in Cuts after three months.

With his daughter married, with the gatekeepers dismissed, Monsieur Vialatte had no alternative but to lodge me under his own roof. He did so, by the way, with good grace, for in between the failure of one maneuver and the preparation of the next, he was the best man in the world. What with the welcome I received, I soon forgot my thirteen-year-old's distress.

Of the weeks that followed I preserve a fond memory. I roamed at will through the vast house, which until then I had seen only from the outside. The sinister gatehouse was closed up. A few days and I had ceased even to remember that I had lived in it for thirteen years. Once I was admitted into the house, the old servant woman forgot all that too. I was Monsieur Vialatte's son.

There, one morning, stood Madame Mobecourt. She beckoned to me. I sensed that she was addressing the misfortunate child I had formerly been. Was she the cause of this new decision? Whatever its explanation, several days later Monsieur Vialatte conducted me to Compiègne, to the house of a tailor where, the day after my arrival, I began my apprenticeship.

Much later, Jacqueline asked for me at the shop. I appeared before her with that particular look people have when one goes to fetch them at their work. What had happened? I didn't know. Jacqueline was angry. She thought what they had done to me was dreadful. I heard her say: "Under these circumstances, it would have been better to leave him at Abel's."

Now I see myself in Paris, in a large sunny apartment from which I look out over chestnut trees in blossom. I recall another panorama, that of an enormous city. Marvelous, all of it. Sometimes I wonder what is about to happen to me. I am told to wait. One evening I am driven in a hackney cab to the Gare de Lyon. It is an unending trip that I make all by myself. I arrive in Menton. I had been standing in the corridor since Nice. These creepings back and forth before the Italian border, how slow they were! Nobody was waiting for me on the platform. I was afraid to get off. Yet I could read "Menton" on the station walls. Did several Mentons exist? Was this really the one I was supposed to go to? Leaning out, I at last caught sight of Jacqueline who was stopping to peer into each compartment. I jumped down to the platform with my little suitcase. She had seen me. She walked toward me, her arms outstretched. She hugged me, asked me a thousand and one questions, took my suitcase, led me to the exit.

For a year Jacqueline and Etienne were able to fancy themselves happy. They were not. There is one thing you must not ask of love: it is to transform unhappy natures. You shall understand, after reading these pages, that this remark was not ventured lightly. Jacqueline and Etienne had been unhappy before marrying. Thus they had remained without being conscious of it. They became conscious of it at the end of a year. That was the point at which the problem of my upbringing served as a distraction.

Jacqueline, who had until then thought it her duty to give me the affection I had been deprived of, discovered that what she had to do was arm me for what lay ahead. She had met with very few disappointments in life. Yet it seemed as though she was following the teachings of a dearly-won experience. Although a child, I scented the theoretical element in this education and such was my unwillingness to fall in with it that I became the cause for ever more frequent outbursts of temper. By and by the fatal words were pronounced: *it was too late*. That may have been true. The habits I had formed at the gatekeepers' were no doubt incompatible with those they wished to instill in me. Jacqueline remained patient. Even if it was too late, they must try to straighten me out. She substituted severity for persuasion. Then she employed her husband as a bogy. What a psychological error! He would take my side, encourage me as soon as his wife left us alone, with the result that I began to idolize him. Wrongly, what's more, for when Jacqueline became aware of this, I underwent the deception of seeing myself betrayed by Etienne.

Another year went by. I was beginning to live inside

[59]

myself. Time, which strengthens friendship, was slowly killing what I felt for Jacqueline and Etienne. It was as if I were discovering as I grew up that they were not my parents. This was unfair. Jacqueline had not taken me away from a deeply devoted mother. It was I who had gone to Jacqueline. They enrolled me as a day pupil in a private school. I interpreted this as proof of indifference. I became unresponsive. I bridled at the slightest criticism. Jacqueline was clearly at loggerheads with herself. Once she said in front of me that it was folly to want to make for the happiness of a child who wasn't your own. She had known neither my father nor my mother. Who was to say I was not afflicted by mysterious defects? So she was waiting until I was old enough to earn my living. Until then, she would do what she felt was required of her.

The war interfered. Etienne, called up on the first day, was killed in September of 1914. I saw his grave years later. It is located among ten or so others in a wheatfield near Château-Thierry. Not a tree, not a ditch, not a hole for shelter; a true battlefield.

Jacqueline returned hurriedly to Paris. I remained alone with the servant in the little house on the hillside. I was sixteen years old. In October I received the order to register as a boarding pupil in the lycée in Nice. I was asked to give the servant her wages, to close up the house, to mail the key.

I kept the wages, pocketed the registration fee, and I struck out across France, dauntless, extraordinarily conscious of my freedom.

It would seem that adventure leaves as few traces in an adolescent's memory as discipline. Two years of wandering about, of inconsiderate open-handedness, imprudent associations, confused aspirations, nights spent out under the stars, today strike me as hardly any richer than the two previous years spent at the desks of the boarding school in Menton.

After Marseilles, Lyons, here we are in Paris. I was seventeen and a half. Where should I go? Over to rue Saint-Jacques, to that hotel with its sides propped up by timbers, the one at the corner of rue des Feuillantines? My mother, so I had been told, had lived there fifteen years before. That constituted a reason for a young man alone in the world. I roamed the streets. The war seemed due never to end. Returning one day from Versailles (I was drawn to all those places where I thought I had moorings), I decided to join the air force. Earlier, at the château, sitting beside a woman—who was that woman?—in the embrasure of a pair of French windows, I had watched the planes, full of admiration. What time was it? What was the weather like? What money was I living on? I returned to Paris. Night was falling. That was when I announced excitedly to my female companion that I would be a hero. The next day, life took me in hand again. How much I would have liked both to love and to be loved by those countless women deprived, so it was said, of love! Those living on ground floors struck me as most accessible. It would have been so easy to enter their places, and to leave, without compromising them! And among such women—I wonder why—, those who gave piano lessons. "Lady gives piano lessons." These words, on small placards affixed by sealing wafers as brightly colored as ribbons, had come at last to appear to me like a disguised invitation. I imagined them, those piano teachers, beautiful and stern. How I would have loved to wait, in a remote room, surrounded by treats, for the lesson to end.

Enough of this childishness.

Warnings precede grave events. I had not paid a hotel

bill—at which hotel? They intended to turn me out. I refused to leave. "You have no right to throw me into the
street without a penny." I imagined I had all sorts of rights.
I had a particular weakness for conscientious objection. For
example, I already knew that, once inducted, I would not
let them vaccinate me. "We're going for the police," they
replied. This threat put an end to the quarrel. But the word
police had been uttered. Before long I would hear it again.
Yet I had not killed, nor stolen, nor even insulted a representative of the authorities. I did not very clearly see where
the wrong lay in what I was charged with. I did not understand why accepting money from a woman who engaged in
prostitution was a misdemeanor.

Eighteen is such an awkward age! You know nothing,
you see nothing, and yet you are a man. I was constantly
hearing that it was enough just to knock on any door in
order to obtain work, and I found none, that it was enough
just to glance at a woman for her to speak to you first, and
they all turned up their noses and walked past me.

That kind of stupidity, by denying me entry into the
thick of life, also kept me out of the way of dangers I was
not big enough to cope with. Had I not even gone so far as
to try earning money in a manner too shameful to name,
strolling on boulevard de la Madeleine, like a woman? It
would seem that my heredity was not as decisive as
Jacqueline had claimed, for I was quite unable to put my
plan into action. Although I walked up and down the boulevard for three nights in a row, not one occasion presented
itself to me. I doubt whether those for whom obtaining a
job or a woman's favors was mere sport would have wasted
their time, as I had done.

Then I thought anew about enlisting, this time in the
infantry (I had forgotten about the air force). It is hard to
believe, but I was unable to succeed. I navigated in a fog. I

went to the wrong offices. When, finally, I got to the right place, I could not even produce my birth certificate. I wrote to Cuts. I never received a reply, I am absolutely certain of that. I wrote to Madame Mobecourt, also without result. Two months later I was still expecting to receive replies. I was afraid to write a second time. Why? What then were the ideas that I had about my fellow beings, about myself? One would think that I must have been timorous, uncommunicative, silent. Not at all. I was a talker, even too much of a talker. I was brazen, vain. I had turned my life into a saga. How much I liked a given person depended upon how much stock he put in my words. Yet I never mentioned Jacqueline. I dreaded her, when it came down to it. One especially self-confident day, I came out with the story of our life in Menton. An Italian man, my senior by I don't know how many years, was listening to me. "You can't leave that house abandoned that way." He convinced me that we should look after it. We took the train. He forced the lock. Yet another danger I came through!

I went back to Paris hidden in a trainload of soldiers on leave. Their extraordinary camaraderie revived my desire to enlist. I wrote more letters. It may be that an underlying prudence held me back. Unless it was that, my involvements in life having just begun, I could not bring myself to leave it. Since in any case I would be called up when my turn came, I could, after all, without shirking my duty, take advantage of the delay granted me owing to my age.

The women on boulevard Saint-Michel attracted me. To me they looked more beautiful than the others. But they paid no attention to me, and it hurt, for I wanted so much to please with my looks. At last, one of them, I don't know why, perhaps because she was in point of fact among the least beautiful, perhaps because she did not consort with other women in her category, took a sudden liking to me. She was a tall, thin person, whose low-cut blouses made up only incompletely for her want of bosom. She had family in Brittany. I dreamed about taking the train, about the two of us living out there, as lovers. In the evening I would wait for hcr in her room. I would fall asleep. In the middle of the night she would return. How strange these awakenings are for the man! And how changed it is, the flesh that offers itself to us as we come forth from a sleep in which we had forgotten about it!

The War! What it costs me to make this confession! I did not fight in it. Was this a punishment, or was it Heaven protecting me? For a long time I thought it was Heaven protecting me. I arrive at the divisional depot, and it's the armistice. But is this not somehow indicative of the mediocrity of my destiny? I could have been exposed to death without providence abandoning me. I could have returned glorious from the war.

So I shall not talk about things I have not experienced. I shall simply say a few words about the time I spent in the army. I meant to enroll in an officers training program. How could I have imagined that at nineteen you are already a subject for inquiries and investigations? Among all the military stripes the one I most coveted was the officer candidate's, with its narrow piping. I took a dictation test. I did a problem. I was already enjoying certain privileges when I had to return back into the ranks. I still remember Captain Laîsné announcing the news to me from where he sat upon his horse during an exercise drill, I remember my shame, his reassuring words, then my tears.

Shortly afterward, I received a letter from my mother. How did she know my address? The gendarmes had called upon her. Why? She was asking me for an explanation—

asking *me*! How difficult to understand all this is! How, as one seeks to remember them, events seem incoherent once one has forgotten the peripeties that connect them!

From that moment on my one thought was of getting out of uniform. My mysterious record followed me every-where. It barred me from the howsoever modest posts I cast about for. It was the ordinary attendant who prevents you from entering. From five to nine, during the four hours I was off duty, I skipped off into the civilian world, where I planted stakes for the future. Indeed, I resembled one of those sorry soldiers who, after parading proudly before the defeated populace, proceed to fraternize with it. I was convinced that only with the aid of someone's sincere af-fection would I be able to take my first steps back into post-army life. Thus supported, I would dare show my face again before Jacqueline, before Madame Mobecourt. A normal life would then begin for me. What did I mean by a normal life? I didn't know. Let me be rescued from all material cares, and the rest, after that, would be of lit-tle importance.

It was in a town in eastern France, some months after having been, as they say, restored to civilian life, that I became acquainted with Germaine. She was a postmistress and the daughter of a local farmer. She was four years older than I and to this day when I think about her, I am re-minded of this disparity in age. Her father would send her baskets of cherries. She herself resembled those hard little cherries that are left until the last. She had a family, women friends, personal pursuits. Modest though her existence was, how I longed to be part of it! The tragic thing is that I have always wanted to become like those whom I have got near to, and it is the opposite that has occurred every time, it is they who have become like me. A little before I was discharged, Germaine handed in her resignation, sold the few things she owned, and went to Paris to wait for me. I wanted to enter her life. She preferred to enter mine.

It was seven in the morning when I came out of the Gare de l'Est. They had allowed us to let our hair grow. Mine was too long, just as the leaves strewing the boulevards were too abundant, fallen from trees untended since 1914. I wasn't wearing a detachable collar, and this bothered me no end. Nobody looked at me. It is always this way when we set foot in a new city. Germaine was waiting for me in a room she had taken on rue du Château-d'Eau. I did not want to join her unless I had no alternative. It was too early to go to my mother's. I went into a public bathhouse. I waited an hour for the water to heat. Before starting out on my trip, I had waited three hours in Châlons for my train, seven hours the day before. So now I was about to see my mother again.

She was living by herself in a small courtside apartment in a handsome building on rue Théodore de Banville, owned by the National Insurance Company. Receipts were sent to her by mail. This flattered her. These are practices possible only between well-bred people. From time to time, she would invite a few devoted friends to dine, with a ceremonial borrowed from the foremost restaurants. Often she thought of her childhood, of the forest in Laigle, of her father's hut, but rarely of Madame Mobecourt. What poverty! A poverty so inveterate it was impossible to dislodge. It went back too far. Not even the remembrance of a relative who would have been well-to-do. Neither kindness nor money could do anything to assuage it. And one would have my mother remember someone who had ignored this fact!

I rang the bell. My mother appeared, physically still attractive. The recollection of her sins, instead of inspiring repentance in her, gave her a feeling of security. She knew how to take care of herself now. She knew how to distinguish, in her misfortunes, the share of responsibility that fell to all concerned, herself included. I thought about everything I had been left to surmise about my mother, about that backbiting no one remembered but that I had not forgotten. Above all, I was not to undertake to see my mother anymore. To pay her a visit would have been an act of disobedience. I could not help but notice that today it no longer was.

My fondness for the Fruchauts originated in their not judging me upon appearances. In my past they had discovered the existence of a world into which, later on, I would probably return. Sometimes they poked fun at me. It's extraordinary how from a certain kind of mocking goodness will emanate. Mockery always ruffled me before I met them. Such was their manner of laughing at some of my words and ideas, at my naïvetés, that their good opinion of me remained unaltered.

I had never dared talk to them about Germaine. But they suspected her existence. At my age, it was impossible to hide something. From time to time they alluded ironically to my reserve. When I realized that they knew me so well, how I wished not that I had not hidden anything, but that I had hidden something of which I could be proud!

They asked to be introduced to Germaine. What humiliation! And then what joy when they told me she was charming, but not suitable for a young man like me, that I had duties toward myself, that I did not have the right to sacrifice my life. Nothing is more comforting than those lessons given by people we admire, than the absence of scruple they would demonstrate if they were in our shoes. They called me a child when I declared I could never aban-

don Germaine. It is true that I had not told them everything. They still did not know that she had resigned from
the post office for my sake. Merely to think that their support might fail if they were to learn the truth cast me into
the deepest dejection. "Ah! You never mentioned that!
That's a different story!" How I dreaded those words!

With growing frequency Germaine reproached me for not
accepting, for the time being, a job of whatever sort. I would
darken at this. The fact of being tied down to a regular job,
simply to meet my material needs, would that not be my
undoing? Did I not have better things to do? I was haunted
by the desire to resume my education. To take a degree in
law, in medicine, that alone struck me as worth my making the effort to break out of the rut I was in. I hung about
the Latin Quarter. I bought curricula outlines. But that was
all. I did not have the spirit, above all I did not have the
strength of will, to do more.
  It is curious that the Fruchauts, instead of blaming me
for this helplessness of mine, were understanding of it. I
had the impression that it made me even more likeable in
their eyes. I should say that they formed a vaguely Bohemian family, for whom lofty aspirations coming into col-
lision with reality was the subject of amused commentary.
The mother, as the good bourgeoise she sought to go on
being, remained conscious of her rank in the thick of everyday worries. She did private tutoring, used the term
French family as a lure to recruit boarders from abroad.
The father, so redoubtable owing to his office of deputy
public prosecutor in the Department of the Seine, had lit-
erary ambitions which otherwise rendered him the most
inoffensive of men. As for the children, they were engaged
in a variety of occupations. The son did research in librar-
ies on behalf of a foreign scholar. The daughter had set her

sights on painting and was taking speech lessons. Whenever they spoke about those demeaning problems having to
do with money, about the ire these have from time imme-
morial provoked in the greatest minds, they seemed to me
to have the right. But I, nobody that I was! Oh, the desire I
felt to be like them at such times! Being poor did not matter to me so long as I was poor in a certain way, the way a
student is poor, or a young artist. And if to this day I never
think of that family without a feeling of gratitude, it is
because they had understood this desire too, and because
their good spirits were a source of encouragement for me,
and because they had the rare goodness to believe I was in
the same situation as they. I thought of other reasons for
liking them them. Their insight, so new to me, into the
hidden springs of human behavior. Their pleasure at coming upon a striking illustration of a state of things said to be
widespread and which I was conscious of exemplifying.
Finally, that mockery I was the object of, a mockery that I
sometimes did not understand but beyond which I divined
a more general mockery aimed at those who had brought
me up. For the Fruchauts certainly had had cause to be
critical of the way in which solidarity is exercised within
rich and respectable families.

I had heard a lot of talk in Menton about the liberal
professions. Monsieur Fruchaut would smile every time I
unintentionally revealed how much importance I attached
to them. There he would discern the mark left by a certain
middle class irresponsibility. To bring up a boy to think
highly of those careers, and then, one fine day, to cease to
care a fig for him.

Time passed. At twenty-three we want to be everywhere at
once. We forsake faithful friends for strangers. What we
possess does not count. Monsieur Fruchaut had no idea,

when he said that I ought not sacrifice my life for anyone, what kind of a quandary he would throw me into, for the first person I thought of was him. Suddenly I had the feeling that without some impulsive act our relations would never end. "Let's break it off here, otherwise a few years from now I shall find myself at exactly the same point." But how? There are some friends we part with who later on seem to have parted with us. Would the Fruchauts be of this sort? I began to ponder the consequences of my actions.

One day they spoke to me about a gentleman from Compiègne.

"You should go see him, he can be of help to you," they advised. Ah, those Compiègne milieux, how well we know them!

"And what shall I say to him?"

"Nothing. Talk to him about Compiègne, about Joan of Arc."

How, I wondered, could so vague a subject create a bridge between us?

"It does defy comprehension."

Monsieur Fruchaut gave me a letter of introduction. It looked to me to be of little weight. A word or two from Abel, for instance, would have suited me better. Is it because we need to have known people a long time in order to feel that their intervention will have any chance of succeeding? I did not believe in a lunch or a visit producing any success.

Nevertheless, I went to Compiègne.

"Madame Mobecourt is very ill," the Fruchauts' friend informed me. "Go see her. You will certainly make her very happy."

Three years have gone by. I have broken with Germaine. I have stopped seeing Monsieur Fruchaut. I still run into their friend Mauguière, the fellow they sent me to visit, for I more and more often spend a few days in Compiègne.

I have a need for change. Every year, every six months, I am somewhere else. It's no longer the same people, nor the same houses. And yet there is no difference. It is the same wretched poverty. Within this poverty which is constant and within this setting which changes I am little by little discovering something new. For some time now I have stopped growing physically, but I feel that I do not cease to learn. In the midst of my idleness and my changes of address I am gradually becoming another man. I do not age, I am becoming aware of what surrounds me.

Ah! That visit to Etienne's parents, not at their estate in Cuts, but in their house in Compiègne. Gazes settle upon me, all identical, as if they were those of the same person. They talk to me about Madame Mobecourt. I incarnate the good that she has done.

It is a Sunday afternoon, with a leaden sky, and music in the cafés bordering the forest. What sadness! The air is heavy. There is thunder in the distance. The flies are biting. And we are all sitting in the park. I am the abandoned child, now become a man. So everything has turned out pretty well. . . A little too much importance is accorded to things I say.

I rent a little room in the Gobelins, near the so-called Ville de Lutèce, the neighborhood's large bazaar. "Just fine," I say upon being shown the room, acting easy to please. A room whose one window faces due east, a room where the summer sunlight comes in for half an hour, then does not reappear until the following morning, leaving an empty patch of blue sky for you to contemplate all day long.

I attach no importance to the distinction between furnished and unfurnished. This room is furnished. Were I to rent one that isn't, I would pay less. This acceptance of expenses that could be avoided is madness when one is poor. I do not wish to organize myself in order to spend as little as possible. I do not care what things cost.

And I have taken it into my head to protect lower middle class folk! I hand out advice around me. What advice, my God! In the most modest households they discover they have connections with wealth. They apply to me because, it seems, I know all about it. Back on rue Descartes, they used to apply to Raymond Fruchaut, on rue Descartes of all places, where for one week I slept up in a maid's room on a box-mattress with broken springs. In those days he used to contradict me imperiously. With him not there I take my revenge. He had one shortcoming that I do not have. He always kept the powerful up on their pedestals, whereas I depict them as regular human beings. "They'll understand," I say. "There's always some way to work things out. Above all, avoid making it appear as if it were your due." That is the crowning argument, instantly understood by everyone.

The church in Compiègne was packed. The coffin rested on a mobile platform concealed beneath black hangings. They were burying Madame Mobecourt. I had gone to visit her a few months earlier. She was a very old lady. She had expressed great emotion at seeing me again. She had gazed at me admiringly. I was tall, strong, handsome. Had she not been right after all? Her old woman's eyes, had they not been more clear-sighted than mine? Was it not dishonesty on my part to complain constantly about my fate all the while I possessed this world's most precious treasures: youth and health? But why this uneasiness I felt to see her satisfaction before assets that I did not owe to her? In reality, I was nothing at all for Madame Mobecourt. The years I had spent in her proximity, though they had been the earliest of my life, had for her been no different from

other years. She told me that she was glad to have contrib-
uted to my turning into a man. A *man*—why only this one
vague word? Did youth and health suffice to illustrate that
theory she so cherished: where there's a will, there's a way?
Did she not seem to be thanking me for having understood
that you mustn't let everything depend on those who are
helping you?

Now she was dead, and she left to other charitable ladies
the trouble of aiding other abandoned children. I did not
dare go up to the members of her family. However, I sat
down three or four rows behind them. I gave my face that
look of deliberate solemnity one notices at funerals. And
when I nodded discreetly to anyone, I was mindful to shed
none of that solemnity. From time to time I glanced at
Denise, Monsieur Jules Dechatellux's niece, seated on the
other side of the central aisle, at the end of the row adjoining mine. Like darkness as one's eyes become accustomed
to it, my dark blue suit seemed to become lighter and
lighter. I had the impression that everybody was noticing
that I was not in black, that the hat I kept hidden was gray.
And more and more often I turned my head in the girl's
direction. She coughed constantly. I was admiring her. She
was so lady-like, with her black suit, her fur, her black
gloves, her self-conscious air from which a sort of ignorance of feminine artifice became apparent.

Suddenly I felt a palpitation, the palpitation I feel every
time a stranger advances in my direction. A woman in deep
mourning, whose face I couldn't make out, had just left the
row where the family was sitting. But I was relieved the
next instant. She bent toward my ear.

"Come sit near us," she said to me in a voice loud enough
for others to hear.

I followed her without understanding what was happening to me. I looked up at the woman sitting across the aisle

and our glances met. Her eyes said: "Well now, this is odd. Why are they asking him to change seats?"

I had just recognized Madame Mobecourt's sister at whose home, as a very small child, I had spent several years. Her son had died, that had been three years ago. Her husband, very recently. Since then she had been living in Compiègne. And now her sister had died in her turn. She was going through that strange period in life when death shows its face to us several times in a row, without, for all that, our wishing to distance ourselves from the loved ones remaining to us.

She had not always been on very good terms with Madame Mobecourt. One would have thought it natural that in the presence of death the petty rivalries from the past be forgotten. Nothing of the sort. Almost as old as her sister, she did not consider herself obliged to grieve beyond measure. She had but to fulfill her duty. It was for this reason she had come to get me, in order that I represent all those who owed thanks to the departed for her blessings.

So taken was I by surprise that I did not think that she had troubled herself simply in order to seat me in the row behind her, and I kept close to her side. Gesturing, she got me to understand that I was to retrace my steps and sit down on an empty chair in the second row. I stood for a moment not knowing what to do. Must I disturb all those gentlemen who were watching us without moving their heads? I turned toward Denise with a woeful air, not to make her smile but to show her my perplexity, as if in such circumstances only she could rescue me. And it was then that an imperceptible smile appeared on Denise's face, a smile that was imperceptible to all except me.

I had lost my main supporter at Compiègne. What reason was I going to invoke now for returning to that town? It is under such circumstances that there appears to us what with our feeble means we are able to distinguish of the designs of Providence. I have observed that Providence is not so impenetrable to an attentive intelligence. I had a presentiment of my destiny. It would be neither brilliant nor happy. It would however be marked by a certain pleasant mildness. At the very moment I was losing Madame Mobecourt I foresaw that a feeling more intense by far would replace the one I had had for her. It was probably because of Madame Mobecourt that I had not yet been able to bring myself to make a frank commitment to a course in life. Often a certain situation lingers on even though the circumstances that brought it about may have vanished. A man of my sort will endure the consequences of this to the very end.

After the ceremony I felt more alone than ever. All there was for me to do was to take the train. Yet a light was shining in the distance: Denise. I was not thinking about what I had borne in life, but rather about what I had avoided. A simple slip of the pen had spared me from the war. There had been a lot of them, those discrete interventions on the part of Providence. Denise's presence a few steps away, was that not providential? Whenever I have a fever I get into bed and call upon the mysterious power which, in us, combats illness. Whenever I am undergoing a moral crisis I turn toward a similar power which also defends me. "Will it be possible that Denise and I fall in love?"

I came back to Compiègne. The Easter holidays were my pretext. I had often thought about Denise's glance. Albert Dechatellux, her father, whom I had not seen for three years, questioned me about my plans. I reddened. He was very nice. I had come at a moment when he didn't know what to do with himself. "Well," he said to himself, "I shall see what this young fellow's made of."

"Sit down, sir."

We fell into conversation as if we were old acquaintances. When circumstances permitted, he would cast a rapid glance at me. I waited until he had finished before raising my eyes. What interested him were not my plans but the characteristic signs of my origins, of my upbringing. I was quick to understand that he had apprehended, not my thoughts, but all the false ideas that a social situation like mine had been able to give rise to. Even though he may have heard about me ever since my birth, even though he may have met me several times, he was now getting to know me.

"Go along and see my son and my daughter."

With each beat my heart felt more and more constricted. I was about to see Denise again. She was there, surrounded by other young men and other young women.

She spoke hardly a word to me that day. She had been like someone who has made us a promise. "Just wait. The moment hasn't come yet. Do you not trust me?" I had left. On what excuse would I return? I had had firm handshakes from everyone. Would they find seeing me again natural? Would I be the obtuse individual who does not understand that he is in the way? I had thought about Denise. About her father as well. I had not been pleased with him. Was it because he had had to struggle in his youth, because he knew what life was like, because rich and powerful though he was, he missed nothing of what went on in the hearts of lesser people? I preferred Madame Mobecourt, or even Jacqueline.

A few days later I caught sight of Denise in the great park. Should I speak to her? Should I wait for her to speak to me? Had she seen me? Had it affected her? Superfluous questions, all of them. She was walking along briskly. She felt nothing whatever on seeing me.

"Are you out for a stroll?" she asked when she came within hailing distance.

I felt incapable of replying from so far away. I pretended not to hear. Then I assumed a jaunty air. I had a bad habit. I always assumed a jaunty air with people who, while aware of my situation, disregarded it.

I had to return to Paris. I had to resume my climbing up rue Claude Bernard. I had to present myself anew at the doors of midwives, medical specialists, dealers in gold and gems, and extend discounts in order to induce them to place their ads through me, for I was then an advertising agent, "in publicity," as I used to put it.

I had just, in a single instant, and thanks to Denise, ridded myself of a vulgar and ridiculous habit: that of looking at the women I wished to please as one looks, in a game, at the partner you want to get to play a certain card.

There were streets and avenues in the Paris sky, between the white clouds. Denise was in love with me.

Two years earlier I had the appearance of an injured workman when I would go out marketing in my slippers. Oh, those heaps of daffodils in the stalls! How they gave me the urge to run away! The building on rue du Château-d'Eau was old and dilapidated, despite the Moorish entrance it owed to a one-story bathhouse at the rear of the courtyard. A bedroom and kitchen on the seventh floor at the end of a hall. A divan with drawers underneath, a worn, soiled bedspread. Propped against the pillow, I would spend hours staring at my neighbors' windows.

Germaine had taken to imitating me. Propped against the pillow, she would also look at the neighbors' windows. Neither one of us was made for this life. Does she still imitate me? I believe so. I have never suffered so much as when I was with this woman. And all those memories of intimacy that remain, and that I do not want to think about! That special word she would say to no one but me!

As soon as I was able to, I would board the last car of the Montrouge-Gare de l'Est train, the one for second class passengers. And for the price of one stop I would ride to place Saint-Michel. Each time I was reminded that, for the price, it was one of the best rides in Paris. You have pleasant interludes in store for you in the most trying periods. How I liked the young people of my own age whom I saw studying and laughing on the far side of the fountain! I wondered that they did not claim ascendancy over me, that they accepted me into their group as if I were one of their own—I, who did the cooking for a woman I loathed. I loitered along boulevard Saint-Michel, stopped in front of bookstore windows. On autumn evenings especially, amidst the bustle that coincides with the reopening of school, in the sadness the rain brings on, I would be invaded by despair. I would look at the girls, so beautiful and so free. I dreamt of having a room on rue du Sommerard, rue Monsieur-le-Prince, rue Casimir Delavigne. Isn't that where I should have been living? But then I had to cross back to the other side of the Seine. And at Châtelet, cut off from the Latin Quarter by the court buildings, police headquarters, Notre Dame, the Hôtel-Dieu, I would feel lost. I would walk back up boulevard Sébastopol. The first store was a bicycle shop. Then came Damoy's, Félix Potin's. "If one evening"—I would sing to myself—"you come upon a blonde as you're strolling along . . ."

I would go back to my room. Well, I was at peace there. Dinner, the evening hours, sleep, they all made the next day feel so far away. I had a respite. I could not lose any more ground. Once the day is done, the world is a better place. The struggle is interrupted. Those who do not participate in it no longer suffer on account of their inaction.

How profound can be the impression left by short spaces of time!

This life had lasted only seven months ... Why had I suffered so because of my poverty, suffered from the dinners we used to have with a retired person who lived behind place de la République, from that interminable day spent with Germaine's mother, from hospital visits to a tubercular little girl, from my furunculosis (to be sure, the boils were mine), from a thousand such things?

Denise came to see me in the Gobelins only once. It was a sweltering day. I had taken off my jacket and I felt a little less poor. I was not ashamed of my room. Each poverty has a particular character. That of mine was to appear temporary. In this way it seemed less ugly than others. I remained a man with some fight left in him, still capable of rebelling. However, by mutual agreement, we never subsequently spoke of this first visit, even long afterward.

At the far end of a private garden, a stone balustrade like the one in the Luxembourg.

Lights from the house were gleaming through the bushes. Muted music.

It was like a dream. My timidity had just evaporated. Inside the faint circle of moon gleamed a slender crescent. Three days ago it had been a thread. Denise and I were by ourselves. I did not desire her. No disappointment could await me. It was the most beautiful day of my life. Would such happiness last? Denise, for her part, was in real life. She was really admiring the sky. She was really smelling the flowers. She was really quivering, and I, in the meantime, was filled with elation over not desiring her.

She wanted to go back inside. I had not dared to kiss her,

but I had dared beg her to stay. I lost all restraint. I allowed immoderate feelings to appear.

"We should go back inside," she repeated.

Nobody had noticed that we were gone. We could very well have committed wickedness, since while it is being consummated it is of no interest to anyone.

A few days later I received a note from Madame Dechatel-lux inviting me to come to lunch. I did not know how to reply. I stiffened. I was wild with joy. I accepted.

Everything transpired very simply. Denise's mother was very gracious toward me. When I got back, I burst into tears. I had wearied everyone with my spectatorial manner. At the table I had wanted to make up for it. I had made fun of that spectatorial manner. Then I had made fun of myself.

Paris was deserted. The greengrocers and the milk-shops had no customers. A chilliness reigned there, and the tile floors were damp.

I was living behind the Bon Marché. On the ground floor of my building was a shop run by an eccentric man who, unwilling to bow to common custom, had gathered within a single business everything towards which he had a lean-ing, even laxity, for this store opened and closed at impos-sible hours. I could not have told whether he was an antique dealer, a cabinetmaker, or an upholsterer.

My house was of good appearance. The height and dark shadows of the entry's arched ceiling, the stained glass, blue and rust-colored, of the fragile inner door, the orna-mental shrubs in the courtyard, all gave a strange impres-sion of a place neither public nor private.

I climbed stairs. At each floor larger amounts of sunlight came in. Everything gleamed, giving off a pleasant smell of floor-polish. A thick tasseled cord hung alongside each door. It is thus the objects surrounding us ought to be. They must be independent of what is going on within us, they must abide no matter what happens, they must be like the prescriptions of a ceremony and say to us: see how it is wise to behave with human nature, without which where would be heading?

My mind was not on Denise. I was weary. The fight for attention, the continual fear of having displeased, watching your every step, justifying yourself, defending yourself, answering—how tiring it all is! A feeling of well-being, of security, of confidence fills me the very moment I give up this effort.

The shutters were open, the bed made. The casement windows, both open, resembled a doll's outflung arms. My clothes had been hung up. The washstand, both marble top and shelf, had been tidied. It looked like the room of a serious young man. No softness anywhere about, or rather yes, a little bit of softness, that of the chambermaid who knows her tenant is a gentleman living alone. She had hung up my ties, but the emptied ashtray hadn't been wiped.

I placed my suitcase on the bed, and without doing anything else, I went out again. This room meant nothing to me, and yet I had had to return to it. I am attached to whatever affects me. On the sinking ship I would hesitate over parting with my jacket, my shoes, I would think for a moment of returning to my cabin for my . . . what, I wonder.

Now I was outside. I was in need neither of rest nor of acclimatization. It did not seem to me that I had just got home.

Denise must have been pleasantly surprised when she paid me a visit the next day. I was forever complaining. Now she would stop believing me. This house was altogether suitable. Why did I always see ugliness where there wasn't any? Denise was perhaps right. I might well have that awful failing of imagining that everything in any way connected with me must be concealed.

Denise had feared something. She felt relieved. Beginning at the entrance, the concièrge, who had served in the finest buildings, must have made a good impression on her.

Denise did not close the door.

"I am very glad you live here. I shan't deny that I was a little afraid after what you'd told me."

I gave the room the sort of glance women give themselves, imagining that I was seeing it for the first time. All at once I discovered what Denise was pleased by. This was not a hotel room.

I was from Compiègne. Denise was not forgetting it. Whatever I might have done, ties yet bound me to my town. Denise was anxious that this be so. She was truly admirable. I remembered all my shortcomings, all she had put up with because of me, my angry outbursts, my prickliness, the ready-made speeches about my dignity, about the barrier separating us, my silent spells. She was there, modest, poor. Only her parents were rich. She herself owned nothing. She was like me. Later on, if she wound up in possession of a certain amount of money, would we not have acquired it together since we had loved each other beforehand? Such was the couple we formed in her mind. And what if she were wrong? If, despite this complicity, my social inferiority caused me distress!

"Why did you come today?" I asked.

Perhaps Denise did not love me. She was coming to see me like any other friend. We had not known one another for so very long. My God, why had all these doubts to be buzzing in my head? By dint of desiring I had worn out my capacity to desire. All that was left was me, in this room, facing Denise, at three in the afternoon, in the month of

July. I was calm. Several times, Denise asked me whether I did truly wish her to leave. My answer was yes. She left. Looking back upon them from a distance, these scenes torment me. How could I have been so light-headed? Thinking back on them, I wince still more at my mercurial disposition than at my foolishness. At present I was alone, through my own will. This was truly the limit. In reality, I am honest, scrupulous. The idea that I might appear self-interested lay behind this peculiarity. But I am self-interested. I am unable not to be. There is nobody in this world who is not. Friends might criticize Denise for loving me, but they did not know the whole story.

Mired in the evil humor famous for having sprung from good feelings, I set out for the railroad station. I had meant to seek forgiveness. Denise was so happy, and I so sad. She would understand. Oh, it was appalling, all of it. Nothing lasted, neither anger nor remorse. Allowing Denise to love me under such conditions was to do her harm. I realized this all of a sudden, and I thought about going back to my room. Nothing is stable when you are suffering. How are you supposed to love, to make yourself loved? How not be unhappy in order to arouse sympathy? How not arouse fear? How surround yourself with all the necessary conditions? What if, at the last minute, Denise's family refused their consent? What would we do? What if it was unwilling to aid the turncoat! One day Denise had told me: "They can't do that." But what if they did it? "Oh, let me never find myself in a situation where I am forced to persuade, insist, beg!" I murmured. For all my efforts to protect myself, I sensed I was heading toward that humiliation. "We are going to be dependent on the goodwill of others. We are going to be obliged to do nothing that might displease."

I come to the station. I shall not ask to be forgiven. I shall tell the truth. But was I so much to be pitied? That story of an abandoned boy, an unhappy youth, I was weary of it. How I wished it might not have been mine! How proud I would have been of another past, even a worse one!

I strolled in front of the Gare du Nord. There were still a good many wounded veterans in the crowd. I did not have a rendezvous. I had to catch Denise as she went by, stop her, as I had stopped so many people. It was five minutes before six. It occurred to me that I had long ago begun saying that it was five before the hour when I had narrowly avoided something. At last Denise appeared. She was accompanied by a friend, Solange Vibot. I felt incapable of accounting for myself. I was on edge, I laughed too hard, I talked too loud. Denise looked at me and smiled. No sign on her face of ill-feeling. She had forgotten about me in the course of the afternoon. It was a sort of pretending in order that the time might feel longer when next she thought of me, and her forgiveness easier when next she saw me.

"Let's forget about all that," she said, thereby rendering my explanations pointless.

She thought that if I had spells of bad temper it was altogether excusable. Later on, when I would be leading a normal existence, she was confident I would change.

The minutes passed. All at once, she asked me to accompany her back to Compiègne. Denise would have these sudden upwellings of kindness. When I was the object of them, my joy would be boundless. But sometimes a child playing in the street or a poor old lady were also their beneficiaries. I would then undertake to temper these impulses. This was not out of jealousy, but because of embarrassment provoked by their disproportion. Pleading looks would then be transferred to me. They knew these impulses were exaggerated. They hoped however that I would not check them. I would turn my head away. Afterward, when we were alone, I would give Denise a lecture. And I would feel that I was vile.

What had Solange Vibot thought? It was evident that I was loved despite my least attractive thoughts and gestures. The sort of man I wished to be was truly the farthest one from Denise's mind. The one she loved was a man who did not deserve any love at all. For me there was something comforting in this. This man wasn't such a little fellow after all! I accepted the invitation to Compiègne. Let's let this little fellow live, let's leave him to his happiness. Albeit little, he is perhaps bigger than many another.

Then I reconsidered my acceptance. The same old habit of backing off from my initial impulse. You possess nothing, you live by yourself, you have no home to go to, yet it always seems it requires much thought before you set off. But Denise did not notice my wavering, and I yielded.

Denise and Solange sat down side by side. I had interrupted a conversation. It picked up again. The fire I had been enveloped in as I boarded the train had gone out. I sat quietly. I sensed it would revive shortly, when Solange left us. While they talked, I stewed in my corner amidst my gray thoughts. I had left Paris without any money. Not for a second had I wondered where I would sleep, how I would get back. I still believed that things would take care of themselves, even when it was impossible.

Solange's brother was waiting for us at the station in Compiègne. He was a tall good-looking boy. He was unaware that I had not uttered a word during the whole trip. I did not want him to find out. Of a sudden I began to talk. They listened to me, but I must have lacked naturalness for I soon had the impression they were growing impatient.

At last Denise and I were alone. Our dispute was genuinely forgotten. It was not because of Solange's presence that Denise had said nothing to me in the way of reproach.

*   *   *

Trimmed shrubbery surrounds the Albert Dechatellux property, hiding the basement windows. Four lightning rods. Not one hint of a fruit tree, but pathways, lawns, spreading oaks. Grillwork separates it, not just from the street, but from the adjoining gardens.

I had needed coaxing. I did not wish to intrude upon them. Finally, as I am wont to do, I had given in. I was therefore about to find myself amidst Denise's family. The chief thing now was not to disappoint. Questions would be put to me. Denise reassured me. "Everybody's very nice," she told me. She believed that my presence would pass unnoticed. She did not realize that easy relations of that sort make sense only among members of a given family, or among the closest friends. Monsieur Dechatellux already had the attitude of a man who, indirectly, had done much of benefit to me.

"Have you been here a long time?" Madame Dechatellux asked me without pausing in her knitting, as if some solicitude had stolen into her.

"We have just this very minute arrived, Madame."

My reply was accompanied by a respectful bow.

Was Denise right? I was not interrupting anything, family life was proceeding. They even shut their eyes to the signs announcing the end of the afternoon, for they were not displeased to have me witness the unfolding of their peaceful activities. I must obtain an idea of the gentility of the world I was penetrating into. Oh, it wasn't a satisfaction of pride! The modesty of one and all was sincere. "We are what we are," every mouth seemed to whisper.

Then came the first ringing of the chime. There was a chime there, as there had been one at Monsieur Vialatte's. But this chime was calling a family together, whereas the other one was something exhibited as a curiosity.

[86]

Everybody got up. Each person had something to do before dinner. Then appeared that singular collective forgetfulness. Everyone seemed to leave to his neighbor the trouble of keeping me company, fully aware that the neighbor would do nothing of the sort. Denise, for her part, had genuinely believed that somebody would stay with me. Seeing I was alone, she came back, not without a feeling of discomfort. She had hoped that they would receive me with greater friendliness.

"But you've only now arrived here! Why, I thought you'd been with us since the beginning of the month. That was what someone told me, I don't recall who."

"I was obliged to return to Paris."

"Naturally. When you're in business your life's not your own."

"I met your daughter at the railroad station. She was so kind as to invite me. I hope, Madame, that I am not disturbing you."

"You are not disturbing me one little bit, Monsieur. On the contrary, I am very happy indeed that you have come."

Then it was Monsieur Dechatellux's turn to take me on. Smiling, he had been waiting for his wife to yield him the floor. An immense distance separated us. I had yet to do anything in life, whereas he had not only struggled for the greater part of his, but had been retired from business for ten years already. The presence of a young and attentive man was an opportunity to recall how far he had come. He forgot who I was. He gave way to confidences. It had been a long time since anyone had lent him an ear.

I nodded my head approvingly. Just then Denise walked back into the room. I colored slightly. I felt awkward to be seeking to please someone in front of someone else I was likewise seeking to please

We moved into the dining room. Despite the silverware,

the crystal, the gilded copper centerpiece, an everyday air overspread the table. Did it come from the half-filled carafe of wine, the napkin rings?

Madame Dechatellux sat down opposite her husband. Somewhat forsaken during the day, she recovered her importance at meal time.

"Help yourself, help yourself, please!"

I would never give in when I was offered something I wanted but had earlier declined.

When dinner was over, Madame Dechatellux rose to her feet, swayed. With me it needed very little in order that an initially considerate gesture become obsequious. My manners lacked naturalness. I knew this. Nevertheless I scrambled to take the elderly lady's arm. She offered me her hand. Her husband cast an astonished look at me. He would never have believed I would take such prompt advantage of the confidence he had shown me. He frowned. I was at the point of wondering whether his wife had not swayed deliberately, whether I had not been witness to one of those innocent ruses practiced between old couples. A disturbing chill had suddenly settled over the family. Looking at the lot of them, it seemed that all of a sudden they had some cause to be vexed with me.

Feeling ill at ease, I set to talking. But nothing worked. Madame Dechatellux herself was infected by her husband's coldness. "People are all alike," he seemed to be saying. "And here this young man appeared to be charming indeed." I fell silent. I intercepted a glance from Monsieur Dechatellux to one of the others, a glance that said: "This young man is deceiving us." Must deception then be the rule in life? One of his sons had died at the age of fourteen. They had traveled, consulted all the prominent medical people, they had him undergo all the treatments, and he had died. His father had thought he was doing the right thing. Perhaps this boy would have lived had they not listened to so many people, nor followed so much contradictory advice.

At nine o'clock Denise announced that she was going out for a walk. I was uncertain what to do. How could I simply accompany her out and not let the others think I felt lost once she was no longer there? By leaving the room too, would I not be seen as clinging unduly to Denise? Would I not be revealing a rather unexpected attachment at the conclusion of a quiet conversation?

Fortunately, she came to my rescue.

"Won't you join me, Jean?"

Once outside I felt relieved. It was not yet night but the tall lamp-posts, lost among the foliage, were already lit. The blue had darkened in the sky. The park gates were closed. I could see broad, deserted pathways, lawns, the château terrace where the chairs had been left in disarray.

I had never tried to obtain certain favors from Denise. Our relations had from the first assumed too serious a tone. We had tacitly agreed to wait. So many grave questions remained in suspense that we would have found it unthinkably light behavior to act like ordinary lovers.

I took Denise by the arm. We walked beside an ivy-covered wall. Every ten steps there was a tree almost touching this wall. Between wall and tree there was just enough space for two to squeeze through. I thought how I had often sought in vain for such spots in cities. In Compiègne they were everywhere. The grave, suspended questions had faded from my mind. A new obstacle arose, of an altogether different order. It sprang from within me. It had nothing to do with our situation. I was unable to suggest to Denise that she step up from the road, that we move closer to the wall for instance. I stopped thinking. I came to a halt. I drew Denise to me and kissed her. What an extraordinary kiss! Our mouths, partially open, had come together so naturally.

Then I was ridiculous. I whispered in Denise's ear like a capricious child who would so much like to be granted a permission. A permission! As if it were a question of permission.

Denise enjoined me to go home to bed, to return to the hotel. I answered that it was impossible, without specifying why. "Now don't be silly. You're going to take the last train." This time, it was truly impossible, and I was very careful not to say why.

We were standing in front of the race-track. I was surprised that my words were so forceful. I told Denise that I loved her. She asked me: "Is that true?" I might have not loved her. She believed me. I was believed just when my words served me so well! We retraced out steps. I looked at neither the wall nor the trees. Denise stumbled. A little incident like this always occurs. You are so absorbed that you knock against somebody, or almost get run over. We were so taken up with one another that only some unforeseen event could have diverted our attention away from ourselves. I became all the more attentive. I dreaded another incident. Then we retraced our steps, still alongside the wall. Up until then I had endeavored to combine my sentiments with my desire. "My love is too strong," I suddenly said. "We have been unwise. A moment comes when a man's passion can no longer be contained." I knew this was not true. I was amazed that Denise did not know it. She believed this moment actually existed.

"And tomorrow morning?" she murmured.

A fresh obstacle was arising. It was not about the difficulty of separating at dawn, without being overheard, that she was thinking, but about what would become of me. She visualized my leaving and was petrified. What would I do outside at four in the morning? Where would I go? Would it not be better to wait for the day when we would not be forced to part?

I answered that in the summer dawn is wonderful in the forest, and that I often used to go out and watch the sun come up. She pulled herself together. That allusion to a personal fondness was a blunder. It would have been preferable not to reply, or better still, to have simply said: "I love you." I saw myself beside her. Then I considered the place I occupied in life. Desire had made me lose sight of it. I felt that I was about to sink back into such cheerless reflections that, all of a sudden, I had recourse to physical force. I hugged Denise to me. Second Lieutenant Le Claud must not have acted any differently. I wanted to and Denise did not want to. Nothing remained of our friendship. I was a foreigner, an utter stranger. Our relations now reposed upon nothing but force. Denise lowered her head so that I could not kiss her. She had her arms crossed over her chest. But she did not back away from me. Instinct commanded me to alternate violence with gentleness. I murmured a few words to remind her who I was. She did not hear them. We had taken months to get to know each other. But she did not know who I was anymore. In her turn she hugged me tight.

I was beaming. I strode straight ahead. Day was starting to break. The birds were singing. By the thousand, in every tree, they were waiting for the sun. Half an hour before, when I had started out, a huge moon had been setting. It was a sight whose like I had never beheld before. But I sensed that in a little while, when the forest shadows ceased to shrink, an uneasiness would take possession of me. The acts of love, caresses, the scaling of walls, kissing, night-time departures, were they not the acts of man at peace with him-

self? Could I perform them, inwardly gnawed as I was? I had
forgotten everything. Now, as I walked along, I asked myself
where I was going. I was loved. But if I did not have the
strength to play the game, what would I offer in its stead? A
sincere love? I could hear Richard sniggering: "But anybody
would be sincere in these conditions!" Should I take refuge
in pride? Denise had got the idea that I was a poor young
man. No, she was wrong. Had that been true, it would have
been wonderful. But what was I then?

The previous evening, when I had taken my leave after
dinner, there had been nothing about my coming back the
next day. This morning, as I placed a leg over the balcony,
Denise had insisted that I stop by the house and say goodbye. I had agreed. But at present I was of two minds. "I have
got to shake off my vanity, there has got to be a difference
between the man I am today and the one I was yesterday,"
I murmured to myself. "I have got to relax. I am happy. I
shall show the change that has come about in me."
    I gave a tug to the knob that made the bell ring. Denise
met me at the door. Last night: struggle, kisses, tears. Come
morning: happiness. The house was already ready for company. The disorder of family life had been put in repair. My
discomfort melted away. I looked at Denise. She hid her
agitation in a way that was charming. She blushed, talked
to me about Solange Vibot. She did not dare ask me what I
had done after leaving her. What a delightful moment! And
I had not wanted to come! I really did not deserve to experience love.

Through the window of the carriage door I saw the line of
automobiles halted at the crossing. I had arrived in Compiègne. I had spent time thinking, had weighed the most
contradictory courses of action. Then I gave my hip a sharp

slap with the flat of my hand. Denise was waiting for me.
I wanted to be cheerful, alert, sociable, in a good mood. She
was wearing a suit of gray flannel, had on white shoes and
a kind of beret. She gave an appearance of dressing the way
she wanted despite an old-fashioned brooch, imposed by
her family, which she wore at her buttonhole like some
sportsman's pin. And how was I dressed? I was in the habit
of comparing myself with others, always with disappoint-
ing results. Today, my two-year-old jacket and my recently
bought flannel trousers were embarrassingly at odds.

When I took Denise by the arm and felt its relaxed state
beneath the fabric, I lost my breath for a few seconds. We
had already spent a night together. We could spend others
now, without entreaties, without struggles. White clouds,
with something reared up about them, were hurrying
through the sky. The streets, still wet after an overnight
shower, with their awnings stirring noiselessly in the wind,
seemed to me like rural lanes beside the streets of Paris.

We walked across the bridge. Wherewith the unforesee-
able occurred. Denise abruptly said to me: "Come. This
way." She crossed the street, stopped in front of the office
of the *Gazette de l'Oise*. "Doesn't this break your heart?"
On display was the photograph of a young man, by it a
bow of black crepe. "Already sorely tried among its
younger generation, the Golf Club of Compiègne has just
suffered a cruel loss in the person of André de Somme-
terre, suddenly snatched away while in the very prime of
life from his devoted family and from the affection of his
friends. Loving sport and—which is not always the same
thing—understanding it too, a former soccer team player,
a horseman as well, he had taken up golf and perhaps
sought in it not so much personal success as to keep
abreast of his companions' progress. We loved him not
only for the great promise of his heart and mind, but also

for the sharp wit with which he would expose the pretentious and the foolish."

I had barely finished reading this obituary when Denise pulled me away, as though she suddenly regretted having diverted my attention from ourselves. It was only a week before that I had left Compiègne. She had got me to come back right away, in order that her father, inevitably making a connection between my return and my preceding visit, would guess what our feelings were for one another.

Monsieur Dechatellux did not reproach me with anything. He did not want to be acquainted with me. What he had heard said about me had reached his ears only after having gone about from one person to the next. There had always been a crowd standing between him and me. And lo! this crowd had vanished! And lo! his own daughter was talking to him about me! He continued to ignore me, however. Yet, from certain glances he shot in my direction, I felt that for him I was no longer the remote, insignificant person of days past.

Denise argued the legitimacy of her desires against the stifling atmosphere that surrounded her. She had endless conversations with the women among her friends. None found her in the wrong. Everybody volunteers when the call goes out to defend love against prejudice. Denise did not complain about her family. She spoke in the tone of people convinced that truth is on their side, of normal people who desire nothing other than to live like everybody else.

However, Denise did not feel absolved by all those words of approval. Something was lacking in them. People were too quick to share her viewpoint. They did not sufficiently understand why she was accepting the situation all the while being so perfectly within her rights. They did not understand that, above all else, she did not want to hurt feelings, and that she loved her family.

Would that hostility have manifested itself had Denise fallen in love with a man more to her father's liking? I put that question to her. She did not reply to me, but the next day she made the following remark: "My parents would quickly tire of their ideal son-in-law's demands."

A few days later, a trap was set for me. All the doors were opened. For me there was nothing to be kept secret. I was treated like one of the family. I was invited to unbend, to feel safely at home. Therein lay the trap. For to unbend, to feel safely at home within the intimate circle others make up, is a mistake. A mistake that I committed.

On arriving, I was stiff, intimidated. They seemed to regret having held me at arm's length for so long. An unwonted cordiality surrounded me. I was so thoughtless as to talk about myself. Then a surge of feeling led me to say how very glad I was to inspire a little bit of affection. Monsieur Dechatellux looked at his daughter. There are households, there are families where they make an effort not to exchange glances in front of a third person. Here, everyone was constantly darting looks at everyone else. Denise understood that her father's look meant I had no education. She did not flinch. I plunged straight ahead. She did not know how to stop me. I waxed warmer. I gave out that I shared all of Monsieur Dechatellux's ideas. But he did not exult. His expression remained just as far away. He symbolized the family that stands aside in the presence of love. "Denise, will you be so stupid as to do this to us?" She showed her confusion. It did seem to her such a natural thing, though, to love me the while loving her family.

As regards me, judgment had been reached. I was an imbecile. How had I ever been able to suppose that I would be received like a son?

No one doubting that Denise had decided to get married, diplomacy made its appearance. Ignoring and scorning no longer sufficed. So high was the Dechatelluxes' idea of the group they formed that, even under usual conditions, each would maneuver independently to maintain its unity. They commended Denise. I leapt at the opportunity and pretended to believe they were sincere. I had set my mighty amour-propre aside. I was finally beginning to feel free. I had just discovered that the greater cleverness consists in taking people at face value and not in racking one's brains to discover what they really think. Since I was being treated as a friend of the family, all I had to do was behave like one. Why had I not done so earlier on? Now that I was no longer in fear of anything, I ceased to be a target. Had I not been right to chuck aside my sensitivities, my fears, my misgivings, since my reward was a feeling of deep inner satisfaction? I even brought myself to wonder whether I had ever really been the object of hostility. You do not create a better opinion of yourself by trying to justify your every action. It suffices to be different each day. Today I shall do the opposite of what I did yesterday. Opinions remain what they are only in so far as we ourselves do not change.

The rivalry between the two brothers had apparently been fierce. To the elder, Albert, the father of Denise, certain privileges had fallen by right. These the younger, Jules, the father of Etienne, had arrogated to himself. He claimed he was the more capable. This eventually came to be believed. Despite their rivalry, the two agreed that something had to be done to remove me from the picture. I served as pretext for a reconciliation.

One day Jules Dechatellux sent word that he wished to speak with me. What cunning! Those outstretched arms, that look of delight at seeing me again! He put a hand on my shoulder, steered me toward his study. It was tea time. Guests were playing bridge. We threaded our way between the tables without stopping. Jules Dechatellux had the delicacy to allow the conversation to start of its own accord. Finally he confided to me that his brother might be clumsy sometimes, but that underneath his cold exterior a very generous spirit lay hidden. He had sat down behind his desk. He had the intelligence not to base his superiority on his money, but rather on the cleverness that had enabled him to earn and hold onto it. He looked straight at me. He knew about my life, but he was not the man to make this felt in so cordial a conversation. To get hold of me through fine sentiments was an idea that had not occurred to him. That could have muddled everything. He went straight to the point.

"Do you know who you are?"

There was a question to which, simple as it did indeed seem, I found it impossible to reply. Was he asking about my character or my social position?

"Do you know who your parents were? Your father was a second lieutenant in the dragoons, I know, but he never acknowledged you, and your mother was a decent girl, I'll grant you that, whom Madame Mobecourt had, I believe, taken in."

I protested that such a definition meant nothing. Why always place the emphasis on social background? Could one not simply suppose that I was the son of two persons who had loved each other? Why always this "who was your father? who was your mother?"

Certain people know how to make us understand what they think of us without putting it into words. With flawless objectivity Jules Dechatellux had established that I was a natural child, that I had no family, no station, no means. He had not understood how, in such conditions, I could dare dream of marriage, whether it be to Denise or to some other young woman.

While he had been addressing those speeches to me I had thought about those men who will not put up with the slightest affront. They rise to their feet, they reply. I had not budged. Actually, he was right. What I had heard was true, despairingly true. No personal antagonism was involved here. What he had said to me he would have said to his best friend, granting the latter could have found himself in my situation. I wanted however to get angry. The occasion was superb. But I had become frightened. I was like a woman who is being outraged in a deserted place. If she calls for help, the man rectifies his behavior.

A few days later I made a discovery. I had gone to see Monsieur Albert Dechatellux for no special reason. When you want to get rid of somebody you start by trying to get him to leave of his own accord. I was suspicious. I was taking no notice of the unpleasant allusions. My mind was on other matters. And suddenly it dawned on me that I was commanding attention. What! I, commanding attention? The scales dropped from my eyes, as they say. I understood that I had never ceased to be a center of attraction, that I had lost sight of reality, that I had no reason to visit the Dechatelluxes so often, and that, officially, Denise was nothing to me, neither my fiancée nor my wife.

The thought crossed my mind of returning to Paris at once. But a few hours can take the edge off one's pride and one's fine resolutions alike. I stayed on. I made do with turning over a new leaf, hoping naively that nobody had noticed anything.

*   *   *

The properties belonging to Jules and Albert were located on the same avenue, two or three hundred yards apart. Though we were right between the two of them I had the feeling I had got lost. The sky was a deep blue. The familiar places, thanks to which Compiègne was not an unknown town for me, no longer stood out. I was expected. I had been told: "You'll come tomorrow, won't you?" As though it had been my wish not to come back. We were all equals. There were neither inferiors nor superiors. What a joke! They hardly said one word to me. "You'll come tomorrow, won't you?" Maybe Denise and I had fallen out of love, such at least was their hope. They still had a good many things to tell me. They kept still. Perhaps I was mistaken. Perhaps the Dechatelluxes had the feeling, as I did, that life is not eternal, that each passing month diminishes the menaces life suspends over our heads. Once we are left with but a few years to live, these menaces cannot very well all come crashing down on us.

We took a walk in the forest. I was surprised that the trees still had all their leaves, since in my mind autumn starts in September. The air was so calm that the zigzagging flight of the butterflies had an inexplicable quality. The weather was still very warm.

The steam from the locomotive faded into the night. A drizzle was falling. The windows were spotted. A strange odor of turned milk, of eau de Cologne, of oranges filled the compartment. Saying goodbye, that evening, had upset me. A train station, the rain, you embrace, you go your separate ways. Was everything going to change? In Paris, the Salon de l'Automobile was just opening. I leaned out of the window. We were in love. One day we would marry. How happy must be those who have a family, who stand at the center of a little universe, who if they stray outside it do so with caution. Returning, it is to resume the place held vacant for them. No doubts, no fears. Do they endure heartache, do they suffer, yet their lives go on unchanged even so. They have simply felt the effect of the law that rules us all. And when they die, for all their having to leave their wives, their children, their friends, their possessions, once again they do but feel the effect of the law that rules us all. This evening I was leaving Denise. I was going to be alone. Temptations would assail me anew. In an hour, as soon as I arrived, I would have to struggle against them with all my strength. How privileged they are who, once alone, are not different from what they were in society! I had no desire to go back to my room, to be yet more alone.

But what I so dreaded did not come about. The city's stir, its lights were enough to distract me. I did not look for anyone to talk to. Pleased by this apparent victory over myself, I proceeded home.

It was the next day that I received the following telegram: "Monsieur Dechatellux deceased." A domestic had dispatched it at Denise's request. Not much by way of verb. One could think that this misfortune had not occurred the night before. Monsieur Dechatellux deceased. Just yesterday I had exchanged a few words with him. This word "deceased" pursued me, as though it behove me to find in it some difference from the word "dead," as though this difference once found, things would not be irremediably over with. But no. "Deceased" meant "dead." Albert Dechatellux was dead.

One November afternoon Denise came looking for me. Her family had collected at rue Verniquet. It was two months since I had seen her last. I had kept in the shadows. This situation suited me perfectly. I left Denise to cope by her-

self. The sorrow they were all stricken with caused me to
be forgotten. It did certainly seem that in my relations with
the Dechatelluxes I must never be myself. For now I could
not help passing off my withdrawal as respect for the family's grief.

Denise invited me out for tea. I detained her at my place.
Afterwards I had a painful impression of having behaved
contemptibly. I had the feeling I had taken advantage of her
being free, of there being no one who could prevent her
from marrying me. As we drove along in the taxi, I said:
"What I did is not right." She looked at me with surprise.
When will the most natural acts stop awakening feelings of
remorse in me?

Now that our marriage was inevitable, Richard tried to
wheedle us in order to maintain a controlling eye on what
we were about. This was a bachelor Richard, a Richard who
had nothing in common with the dedicated physician of
the rue de Rome. One day I told him I had no cause whatever to show him gratitude. He took offence at that. We
were in the mood of animals about to lock horns. Denise
had intervened. You blush from shame when you recall
such scenes.

And that way of his of talking about the advantageous
thing to do! That feigning to address oneself to an equal.
"You must be insistent with Denise that she take it upon
herself to sign the transfers, for we are nearing the dead-
line," said Richard who cared not at all about peremptory
pleas. How truly sincere he appeared! "No, Jean (the sound
of my first name on his lips!), you do not have the right to
think such a thing of us," he exclaimed one day when I
foolishly confessed to him that I felt myself an intruder. He
would draw up plans for our future. "You'll return to
Compiègne. In Paris I'm afraid you'll experience difficul-

ties making ends meet. You'll have an office in town, with a fine map of the department in front of you." His idea was to induce the management of an insurance company to shift their general agent in the Oise. I would remain a simple broker only for the time it took to engineer this ouster. I agreed, counting upon this project falling into oblivion. Denise was not any more ambitious than I. Her indifference made me feel uneasy. For I was wrong. The wise thing would have been to live in the way Richard wished. It was he who was right, not his sister, not I.

Sometime later, he announced to us his intention of buying a house in Compiègne. He would rent it to us. It was for us, he declared, that he had decided to invest in real estate, for he was not partisan to this sort of operation. I had yet to find out that buying can be a source of worry. For me it was simple enough: "Either you buy something," I said to myself, "or you don't." Denise and Richard thought the house too expensive, whereas I, with a levity that must have shocked everybody, had mentally subtracted the sum being asked and had given no further thought to the matter.

You are always poor compared to someone. Richard was not aware of this. For the truly rich, there must not be, it seemed to me, a great difference between him and me. I was mistaken. Richard was of their number. He hesitated, waited, chose. Like them he did not fear wasting his time. He knew that by these signs you recognized established wealth. What most surprised me was that so many people had gone into action for sums which struck me as mediocre. I imagined that you bought a house the way you would a suit, yielding ever so little to the salesman's wishes. Although the house was modest, Richard had already made ten trips to Compiègne. And Denise found this commendable. At bottom he preferred handling a piece of business to seeing patients.

I suffered from my inferiority. Richard was convinced that he was the cause of this suffering, that I felt inferior to him. For a long time he struck a pose. He pretended not to know that I was observing him. He would niggle over the payment of an ordinary bill and would affect indifference over a heavy loss. At the point where a certain intimacy came to exist between us he started to play a rather surprising game, that of having nothing to hide from me. He wished to make me understand that men are guided by self-interest alone. He flew into a temper in front of me over an improperly claimed sum. It was understood that I was no better than he and that if I loved Denise, which he did not doubt, it did not make her fortune any the less of an influence upon my feeling for her. How could he have so little self-esteem? I wondered about this until the day he made a singular remark: "You have to realize, Jean, that in our milieu we do not need the approval of anyone in order to act." Indeed, that approval was quite superfluous. I was able to verify this now that I was having frequent occasion to meet Denise's friends. What discretion they displayed the moment a subject of complaint seemed to have a familial cause!

In the spring the Dechatellux family moved back to Compiègne. My apprehension grew as our marriage approached. I did not think it possible that a formality could bring about the changes I wished for. Denise's mother had become very different. She pretended to believe her husband was still alive. Sometimes she spoke of him as if he had just then stepped out. She did not speak however in a way that could raise doubts about her sanity, but the while giving her interlocutor the look of those who lie without the assurance they will be believed. It could be that playing this dotty little game brought her relief. But she had played into

Richard's hands. He had given her a lady's companion who never left her side.

Madame Dechatellux all of a sudden showed a sincere affection for me. What had produced such a change? What mysterious evolution had her mistrust undergone in order to turn into sympathy? Was it age? Turnabouts of this sort are frequent among the elderly. They provide them with the illusion of an independence they have lost. Unless, to take a more generous view of it, a sincere affection had indeed come into being.

When one morning I met Abel on the place du Marché-aux-Herbes, he had not even the curiosity to examine me, to try to grasp what kind of person I had become. Yet it might have been interesting to compare what he would have turned me into with what I had actually become. On I forget just what occasion I caught myself saying: "My father, Lieutenant-Colonel Le Claud . . ." There are events we hold to be certain even though we cannot explain how we know about them. Thus, I was persuaded that my father had obtained the rank of lieutenant-colonel. Likewise I was persuaded that one of my aunts had taken the veil. Nothing could be less sure. But in the situation where I found myself, everything so far lacked solidity that I never hesitated to make a reality out of the vague rumors which happened to reach me.

Jules Dechatellux had become another man since his elder brother's death. The day of rivalries, of jealousies was past. For months he had not seen his sister-in-law, Richard, Denise. I found out that he was in love with one of his wife's friends, a person nicknamed Bébé, and he was preparing to go on an extensive trip.

Richard's idea now was to get his uncle to use his au-

thority to dissuade Denise from marrying me. Was this not
unconscionable on the part of a son who incessantly
claimed he was obeying his father's secret desires? Could
one more breezily demonstrate that behind all those un-
stinting marks of friendship there had been not one iota of
sincerity? I asked myself this question, for in those days I
was prone to trying to fathom the feelings of the people
who hated me. One person had done one thing, another
person, something else. By rejecting this I could obtain
that. By accepting this . . . and so on.

Richard's naïveté was truly infantile. Denise's feeling for
me, he supposed, was superficial. If he was unsuccessful in
bringing her around to reason, it was because he was her
brother, but Jules Dechatellux would know how to get
through to her.

Denise did not allow herself to be upset. She went along
with her brother's wish, though not without declaring to
me that she found his interference grotesque. But life was
continuing. One must not become obdurate, one must not
make enemies needlessly. Such a discussion would serve
to clear up misunderstandings. "After this there will be no
further doubt about the feelings I have for you." What happened at their meeting? It seems that all Jules Dechatellux
talked about was himself. He was a man who avoided efforts of whatever sort and for him the conciliating of two
points of view was an effort. His mind was entirely taken
up with his mistress. Richard had been unable to get a sign
of life out of him. As for Denise, she admitted to having
taken advantage of her uncle's euphoric state in order to
talk bluntly about money. She was fed up with being unable to recuperate what belonged to her. Richard had
sprung to his feet. Yes, his sister had certainly been more
clever than he.

*   *   *

She joined me where I was waiting for her, sitting on a bench by a path in the park. It was weeks since I had felt so demoralized. That discussion seemed to me of enormous importance. Was I not the subject of it? Strollers passed by. They had that air of the very pretty girls who look at no one, who stare solemnly into space. Certain ones had recognized me. They may have been curious to know how I had fared, but they were unwilling to turn their attention my way.

Life is full of these coincidences. While Denise was at the home of Jules Dechatellux, Etienne's father, I caught sight of Monsieur Vialatte, Jaqueline's father. He advanced with little shuffling steps. On a leash he had a very small dog of the sort you find in city apartments. How old this man looked to me! Oh! he no longer thought of chucking his responsibilities. He had been a fool and lost everything he owned. He lived meanly, without servants, in a modest house which the Rivers and Forests Administration let to him for a pittance. He had not wanted to do anything for me. Nor had he wanted to do nothing whatever. And today the city of Compiègne was treating him the same way he had treated me. It had not adopted him, but it had not abandoned him either. I watched him move past, absolutely incapable of recognizing me unless I were to plant myself in front of him. Perhaps I should have stood up. But there was no longer anything between us. He would have forced himself to ask me a host of questions. Why oblige this old man to seem happy at seeing me again?

At last Denise rejoined me. The discussion must not have centered upon me personally. They found me neither more nor less to their liking than anyone else. And yet I sat there, upon that bench, trembling in anticipation of an answer, trying to guess from Denise's demeanor whether it was positive or not.

When she announced to me like a piece of good news that her uncle felt no animosity toward me I was unmoved. This was a politeness on Denise's part, since my name had not once come up. I sensed that it was no longer I who was the source of her preoccupation. All this animation was owing to her having just come from a family conference. Since her father's death she had been acting as though no wrong was attached to the premature enjoyment of what we desired. She was right to feel concerned solely about her kinsfolk, since she was so sure of all the rest.

Manifestations of hostility toward us ended once we were married. Denise was now a stranger. They would be fair, courteous, amiable, since everything was over with. Official ceremonies bring out everyone's true condition with added clarity. I knew this and worried about it. Without my being different, my life, it seemed to me, would stand forth summarized in my person. Our marriage was far from resembling the one Denise had imagined as a young girl. I thought I was the cause of this disillusion. Just when everything is proceeding as if this were a profoundly united couple, how conspicuous do arrière pensées become! And how uncomfortable I felt amid the people around me! So long as only recent friends approached me, I could deal with them. But some loomed up from so far back in the past! Richard, fortunately, along with some of Denise's friends, so as to relieve the strain pretended to make this ceremony the occasion of a good time.

Denise and I were walking down the Champs-Elysées. After the luncheon we had all promptly gone our separate ways. A few words were exchanged out on the sidewalk. Then

Richard had sprung onto a bus. He seemed to be saying: "Now that you've achieved what you wanted, goodbye." He waved to us from the platform for quite some time.

A faint mist drifted over the avenue. We sat down at an outdoor café. An uneasiness arose in us. There was something frightfully personal about our adventure. So we had struggled for so long to obtain only this! We could not complain anymore now, we ought to be satisfied. "Then what else do we desire?" We asked ourselves this question in order to mask our uneasiness. It was a good thing that Denise who, married for an hour, had felt the need to let herself go, to feel protected, now pulled herself together.

Parisian life seemed to unfold before us as though for the first time. Everything about it was gay, lively. You sensed its readiness to come to the defense of the innocent, its inherent good spirits. Evil made its appearance there only accidentally. And as for us, here we were, side by side.

We watched each other live. Every day, like the adolescent who, after his first sexual pleasure, wonders whether he will not experience still greater ones, we would wonder whether something unexpected was not going to occur tomorrow. We revelled in our intimacy. Then came the moment when we ran out of things to say to each other.

When we saw *our* family again, it was just as if we had never left it. Madame Dechatellux even showed great joy. Reprobation was kept perfectly concealed. They found a cruel pleasure in making us believe that nothing had changed. Denise detected nothing. She was touched. She was even visited by remorse. She thought that she had been unfair to her family. When eighteen months later Richard married in his turn (he was to become another man under the influence of his strange wife, whose maiden name was Fondelaire) her family's indifference towards her could no longer escape her notice. Nobody had consulted her. She had not been admitted to the conventicles which precede nuptials. Wanting the same for others that she had wanted for herself, she had loudly approved. But she had been made to understand that this marriage had no relation to her own, and that the general approval rendered hers unnecessary.

Despite this coolness we returned often to Compiègne. We were kept at an ever greater distance. People who fall out with each other always dream of great successes—not the Dechatelluxes, however. A heavy atmosphere reigned throughout the house. It seemed that Denise was held responsible for it, that because of her a pall had been cast over her mother's golden years. A rancour of the forsaken partner hovered in the deserted rooms, without that causing anyone to cease pretending he had lived life to the hilt. They talked to Denise about imaginary journeys, new relationships, plans. They had even stopped going to the trouble of telling her the truth.

The years went by. The comforting feeling of beginning one's life afresh does not last. Man is not built to delete the past and start again from scratch. Instead of living a new existence, I little by little realized that I was continuing my old one. And I made this discovery just when Denise and I became indissolubly united. What thus bound us together was neither love nor marriage, nor the struggle we had waged together, but the extraordinary abandonment that would overtake us were we to separate. The Denise I had seen laughing among her friends, the Denise I had seen in the bosom of her family, would she be able to endure such abandonment? Was this not the story of Germaine all over again? The one had left the post office for my sake, and the other, her family.

*   *   *

We knew a day would come when we would run out of money. And now all of a sudden that day arrived. For all our having foreseen it, it took us by surprise. What had happened? Nothing. It was exactly like what happens as regards age. There was now nothing to do but regret. As the saying goes, all we had left was our eyes to weep with. We ought to have done either this or that. Yes, but it was too late. We were without any resource at all. The quarrels over the securities remaining in the family's joint possession grew more acrimonious, but were not settled. Hidden behind Denise, I was in a humiliating situation. I must admit that nothing was said against me, at least not to my knowledge. They must have viewed me as irresponsible, which allows me to think that in the final analysis the wicked do not use all the weapons at their disposal.

As she was unable to gain possession of certain stocks and shares due to come to her, Denise reported her brother's dishonesty to all and sundry. Everyone sided with her, as they had done in Compiègne when she spoke of marrying. Stories had to be listened to about how things were done correctly in other families. Everyone offered himself as an example. Our father had specified thus and so. When our mother died, this is what we did. As the eldest, this is what I said: "You wish me to draw up the partition of real goods? I shall hand a copy of it to each of you. You shall examine it. You shall consult your notary, your lawyer, whoever you like. If you have an objection, you shall raise your objection. As for the objects that cannot be divided, those to which we all ascribe a sentimental value, we shall draw straws for them."

I was treated to descriptions of other, equally perfect ways of proceeding. I was finding it more and more unpleasant to listen to this. I myself leaned towards temporizing, concessions, private bargaining. I do not claim to be an especially sensitive man, but those disclosures of family dealings deeply shocked me. Denise stilled my scruples. I knew nothing about such things (she was right). Figures were figures. Not only did accounts have to be exact, but they had to be settled swiftly. That was an elementary rule. From all evidence, I was unacquainted with any rule. One proof of this was the humiliating to-do about the overcoat I had borrowed but forgotten to bring back the following day, the anger of Denise's friend at whose home I had however spent a pleasant evening.

I stood aside. True, my intervention was not required. Once, however, when Denise and I were alone I dared insinuate that things need not be the same everywhere. In the Fruchaut family, for instance, I had never noticed any such disposition to greed. Denise gave me to understand that I did not know what I was talking about. Everywhere it was the same way. I did not persist. "It's only little people," she concluded, "who don't bicker over money." I said to myself that after all she might well be right, and the Fruchauts, whom I had rated so high, fell in my esteem. Yet they got along so well. Henceforth I took care not to cite their example. But I was not convinced. When large sums are the bone of contention, it is admissible that some within a given family stand up against others. As concerned Denise, though, this was not the case. The clash was over something on the order of twenty or thirty thousand francs.

How uncomfortable it made me, in the midst of our difficulties, to hear Denise talk about her safe-deposit vault, about her investments manager, about her bankers! I confessed it to her. Her astonishment was such that I realized that the habits wealth engenders do not disappear when it does, that our present distress, while identical in its consequences to the distress I had undergone, did not resemble it at all in any other point.

In the Mademoiselle Vialatte era, I had been, according to Denise, neither a child of middle-class parentage nor a working man's child nor even an adopted orphan. I was beginning to think that this assertion rather hit the nail on the head. For instance, while observing how Denise's cousins lived, I had come to see that the upbringing Jacqueline had given me (one I thought so exceptional, which is understandable when you have lived until the age of twelve in a gatekeepers' lodge) bore no comparison with theirs. Those boys enjoyed the liberties of adults. The teachers before whom I had trembled for so many years inspired no fear in them. They spoke of them as their parents' subordinates. It was thus that, little by little, Jacqueline's prestige had sunk in my eyes. She had inculcated in me what she knew, but she did not know a great deal. To her I owed some strong ideas, like that of personal responsibility. But when combined they formed a contradictory whole. I understood what Denise meant in saying that I was neither the son of someone from the middle class nor a working-man's son. I was an ignorant young man, neglectfully raised, who, thanks to what he was being allowed to see today, was gradually gaining in refinement.

I resolved at last to return to the advertising agency where I had worked seven years before. Denise had several times expressed a desire that I do so. Whenever I had left it was like a man who never intends to come back. And now Denise had asked me to perform this about-face! And she considered it natural that I do so! She had no inkling that this was harder on me than getting myself taken on as an unskilled worker in a factory, for instance. From her unexperienced person's viewpoint, the only thing I had to overcome was my pride. "It is never dishonoring," she would repeat, "to ask for work, even from people we know."

René Gallu, my former boss, was not in his office. I questioned the concierge. He informed me that Gallu usually lunched at the restaurant next door. There was in the reconstituting of his daily habits something that brought my past wretchedness back to mind. Suddenly, from where I was sitting, I saw René Gallu through the window, standing in front of the restaurant. He kept changing his mind about whether to enter. He was talking to one of his brokers, just as in the past remembering, every time the conversation seemed over, that he had overlooked something. Noticing how this inability to wind things up grated on me, I realized that good will by itself is not enough when you wanted work. You needed patience also. Finally, in he came. He was still elegant. He was wearing the classic double-breasted dark blue suit with white pin-stripes, a lavender shirt with attached collar, a tie that he apparently did not consider too garish, and a rectangular wristwatch with heavily drawn numerals. The narrowness of his Croix de Guerre ribbon did not denote scorn for decorations but went along with vestmental modesty. He was holding his hat in his hand. His hair still had its glossiness. His closely shaven cheeks had that bluish cast which in other days you used to notice among actors. On finding René Gallu so much like what he had been before, an uneasiness came over me. The years I had just lived had been lived by him too. So he had learned no lesson from them. So he had simply done his best to stay the same. A little later I decided that this impression some people give of being immobile is deceiving. We believe they have vegetated just as we believe that the agricultural workers we see from a train are sunk in boredom, but it could be that they are more self-contained than we.

I had imagined that Denise was genuinely eager that I resume my job. Great was my surprise when, upon my return, I discovered I had been wrong. Had she suddenly grasped the underlying reason for my aversion? No, the truth was entirely different. She had heard so much disparagement of me that she had finally exclaimed: "Very well, since this is the way things are, Jean will do nothing but what pleases him." Had the partition of her father's estate been carried out honestly, I seemingly would not have been obliged to go back to work for Gallu. "Jean has no reason to bear the consequences of my family's nastiness and nonsense. He is my husband. When I married him he had no situation. I was perfectly aware of that."

A few months later, Denise had the idea of paying a visit to her aunt and her mother's sister-in-law. As far back as she could remember, she had heard only disdainful things said about these two women, and so it was that when we were married it had not even occurred to her to notify them.

And now she was preparing to go see them. Upon my advising against it she expressed surprise. No one could possibly know less about how society works (that perhaps was why she had married me) than she. The idea that people would think she was less proud because she was in trouble did not even enter her mind.

Strangely enough, neither the aunt nor the sister-in-law ventured a connection between Denise's unexpected visit and her situation. Their unfortunate coincidence did not escape them. But Denise so obviously did not see what this coincidence could lead one to suspect, that to appear to have it in mind would have been to show a very mean side of oneself. They were wholeheartedly with her. They gave her to understand that they had always made a distinction between her and her family. They found Richard's conduct abominable. However, prudence bade them to appear to be standing above the fray. These women had things they could say about Albert Dechatellux. They took good care not to utter them. He was dead. Let him rest in peace. Then they spoke of those qualities of the heart that alone count in life. They wanted to show that perfect union was not the privilege of the Dechatellux family. And when they made bold to talk about me, it was to say that I was certainly a charming man, that I did not deserve all the vexations I had been subjected to.

But in vain did they behold right to be on our side, in vain did they consider that in as much as we loved each other we had no need to concern ourselves about others, Denise was left with the feeling that they understood the family's point of view.

Oh! resentment had not blinded them. You would have said they had never suspected that they might have been shunned. And when they were led to give their opinion the two sides of the scales they held were ostensibly even.

They never did anything else. I was wary of saying this to Denise. Just as she had not been alive to the illogicality of her visit, so she had not anticipated the uproar it would cause. At present Denise's two relatives were in consultation, going here, going there, relating what had happened. No one denied that Denise had fine qualities. These were even exaggerated as they sought to appear to have no part in the miserable tittle-tattle beginning to go around. Denise had a heart of gold. Her husband didn't seem to be an evil person. Of course, he wasn't well off. He left it to his wife to dig them out. He was, so the story went, the son of a sergeant-major and of a chambermaid. Here was the once-in-a-lifetime occasion to pay back that snooty Dechatellux family in their own coin. But have a care. Stand behind Denise and they ran the risk of being lumped with her, of justifying the estrangement they had suffered from and of which they wished, through a well-maintained neutrality, to show the injustice.

"How is one to help them?" all these people wondered. Knowledge of our misfortunes had come like a bolt out of the blue. Consequently, it was difficult to palliate them with little bits of financial assistance, as was usually done when the situation had been common knowledge for some time. People recalled that if Denise had excluded herself from her family (that was how she herself put it), she was a charming person nonetheless. So one had to intervene. To arrange a meeting they sent her an enigmatically brief *pneu*, for these people, the moment they departed from their day to day life, would cloak themselves in mystery, no telling why.

Denise went to her aunt's, again despite my wishes. After a lengthy preamble she was asked to think about what might be of help to her.

"You were right," Denise told me when she returned. But it did not occur to her to wonder at such hesitation. She even felt a certain gratitude toward her aunt for having given her a cordial welcome. She did not want to admit that she had been expecting some assistance from her relative. And so that there might be no doubt on this point, she subsequently compelled herself to visit her regularly.

When later on, illness having forced her to take refuge in Compiègne, it could appear that Denise had made peace with her mother, that aunt and that sister-in-law forgot what had happened. They made no use of the advantage they had gained when Denise confusedly awaited some support from them. To maintain relations which had developed thanks alone to this situation, they judged it a clever move to seem not to remember anything.

*   *   *

At this point a dreadful event occurred. Our future hinged on Madame Dechatellux's death. It was forgivable that this be so for Denise's future. But for mine! At the beginning I did not realize what was going to happen. I attributed to impatience the hurry I would be in to hear from Denise about her visits to her mother. No other reason could have occurred to me. I was far and away from having my advantage in mind. Denise knew this very well. I had come to like Madame Dechatellux a great deal. If for a long time she had displayed toward me the condescension of a patroness for a deserving young man, I had very soon detected the childishness of this pretension.

Today I could no longer hide the truth from myself.

I had believed that I was never again to find myself in a situation which for baseness resembled what I had experienced when one evening I had sauntered up and down boulevard de la Madeleine until one o'clock in the morning. Since then I had not known the feeling of shame, and now I was feeling a shame worse than all I had known hitherto. I had believed in my victory! What an error! Depraved habits fade away on their own, and if you are not clairvoyant you can attribute to yourself the merit for this. But they disappear only to recur in a different form, as is said of diseases. I was attacked in a sector where I no longer thought to maintain my defenses. How could I have been reduced to wishing for someone's death? "Wishing" was not the word. I did not wish for Madame Dechatellux's death. I did not desire it. It was worse. I had let events develop in such a way that this death would straighten out everything. That is how I had been caught. I had believed that to be a man you had to live in accordance with your conscience. And all of a sudden I had the revelation that this was insufficient. And this revelation, like the preceding ones, came too late. Oh, the ever new lessons life teaches me! I had felt that my youth was an abomination that had to be concealed from everyone. Then I had naively convinced myself that with each passing year my youth lay farther behind me, so that I could now allude to it lightly, without one knowing whether I was being serious or ironic. I had convinced myself that never again would I relive the suffering inflicted upon us, not by poverty, for poverty is without importance, but by the shame we feel before our thoughts, our acts, our very selves, and lo, I was reliving it more violently than ever in the past. I was at least able to tell myself then that society had its share of responsibility. But now!

I no longer dared come within Madame Dechatellux' sight. At the sound of her name, I would lower my eyes. And this was the moment when we were forced to return to Compiègne.

Denise had a fever. Was this my punishment? I felt dizzy. Richard, whose hand I refused to shake, became my savior. My God, why was it not I who had the fever? We could no longer pay for anything. Down upon us they came: the rent, the gas and electric bills, shopkeepers' bills, threats of seizure. You sink only little by little, which had given us time to try everything. To us no means remained for extricating ourselves from this hell. We left our rue Pergolese apartment, taking the key with us, giving no forwarding address, leaving everything in a repulsive state. "Let her die," I pleaded, "so that all this may come to an end and such torture never begin again!" But as I have said, my destiny was marked throughout by a certain mildness. When Madame Dechatellux died, I had stopped wishing for her death. I had lived close by her for several months. I had spent quiet evenings close by her. I had understood that she was a living being.

*   *   *

I drifted about freely in the big Compiègne house. I opened doors which, in the past, had been closed to me. I was a foreigner, but the years had worn many things away. We had come together despite the differences in the start we had each had, that start that you must not miss, as Madame Mobecourt used to say. I would wander up to the top floor, and Richard, if he ran into me, showed no surprise. They took a perhaps exaggerated interest in my tastes. I was struck by this, for I was not accustomed to lend them any importance. Richard still did not care for me, but he no longer disdained, as has gone back to doing, the little satisfactions that my presence afforded to his pride. Among these was the favorable idea I was being given of daily life in Compiègne. If I needed some object, for example one which his wife happened to be using, he would insist that she hand it to me. It seemed that I might have some catching up to do in my material well-being.

Every month Madame Dechatellux would fall ill. Because of her asthma she was not to stay in bed. She would begin her convalescence right away. She would walk inside the house, taking little steps. I would come across her sometimes, and I was struck by her look of concentration while performing so simple an exercise.

Denise was still feverish, but I was not so afraid that something might happen to her. She had her family around her. For years she had declared that she would rather die than ask her family for anything. And yet she accommodated herself very nicely to this hospitality. She seemed happy. There was no glorying on anybody's part and nobody felt humiliated.

Following her last attack Madame Dechatellux lingered in her convalescence for as long as possible. Is it not while convalescing that an ill person feels most sheltered? And long after her disease, in giving fresh signs of virulence, had shown that the period of quiet had passed, Marie-Antoinette Dechatellux still imagined she was deriving benefit from some sort of prescription and that it would be given to her to see the rose bushes come into flower out on the terrace . But death overtook her, depriving her of only this modest desire. She was sixty-eight years old. She had hoped to go to sleep and not wake up. Everyone had believed it would happen, she had become so frail and feeble. But her agony had lasted for forty-eight hours, and was horrible. Farewell seasons, carriage outings, picnics, farewell convalescences, the charming company of the children!

Denise had been bedridden for two weeks. For the first time I had the impression that she might not get up again. We could have been so happy now.

We looked at one another in church and we did not recognize one another. Upon returning from the cemetery I was introduced. Pressing my heels together, I performed a slight bow, something halfway civilian, halfway military. The colonel did likewise, with an added nuance of respect, warranted solely by the fact that I was the son-in-law of the deceased. After moving off I stopped and turned around. He did the same. Later on we found ourselves sitting together at the table.

A sort of tightness in my chest prevented me not from breathing but from eating. The peacefulness descending from the cold blue sky I saw through the windows was hurting me. Nobody cared about the beautiful weather. It was two o'clock in the afternoon. I was unsettled. It was becoming harder and harder for me to stand away from my habits. We were unable to recognize one another. A human countenance does not remain engraved in the memory for fifteen years. The color of the hair, the shape of the face grow dim. Our eyes kept meeting more and more often, however. We would have liked not to be sitting across from each other in order to query our neighbors. Then, all of a sudden, we recognized each other.

I was trembling now, my head lowered. My shoulders felt narrower. Was Colonel Laîsné going to speak? A day passed, he did not speak. Why? Was it because we attach little importance to the pain we have come to be acquainted with in the exercising of our profession?

How I wished that Denise would get well, that we could escape from here! Is there a torture more awful than to remain bound to one's faults through the illness of a loved one? It was possible, after all, that the colonel had spoken, that it had been kept from me because the moment was grave.

Denise was dead. Richard was keeping vigil, seated at her bedside. He held his head in his hands. He seemed to be sleeping. Both looked as if they were on a voyage. I stood motionless in the overheated room. I had not known that Denise was sick. For years I had lived with her and never suspected it. When she would cough, when she had a temperature, when she was obliged to stay in her room, I would take care of her, I would keep her company, I would entertain her, but I did not know she was sick. In the warning signs her illness gave off I saw nothing anticipatory of death, for to death I had never given a thought.

Denise died at the age of thirty-three. She did not seem like a victim. Her destiny was wanting in not one of life's principal events, those at least whose dates are given by biographers. She had been born, she had known a happy childhood, youth, love, marriage, and she had died. Yet there she lay, in front of me, as though she had not lived.

All the ceremonies of existence, she had celebrated them, and she wanted to keep on living.

I wept. The nurse looked at me. Until that day, like her, I had looked at the unhappiness of others. Today, for the first time, I was looking at it no longer. It was I who was being looked at.

My legs were ready to give way. I sank into an armchair. By now I was alone in the bedroom. I contemplated Denise. The feeling of release lay upon her features. The paraphernalia used in caring for her was still there, without purpose. I did not take my eyes off Denise's face. In that serenity no place existed for me. This afforded me an immense relief. Heaven had spared me the greatest grief of all, that of seeing a loved one struggle against death, not in order to live, but in order to remain near you. Once Denise's state had worsened she had ceased to recognize me.

I got to my feet. I walked out of the room. I had been there with Denise the whole night. I was not able to remain with her any longer, at least I was not able to in the view of other humans. Long ago I had noticed that they are very quick to judge us at the end of our strength. I could have remained there beside Denise, I could have left her only after she was placed inside her coffin, I could have not let go of the corner of the sheet I had been clutching in my hand for hours. What was the use? I hid those four words away in the depths of me. Had people read them in my face, what would they have not imagined? I am a monster. I have never loved Denise. And I am escorted with no end of consideration into another room.

Now I remember that I had cried forth from pain as I have cried only three or four times in my life. As I did so was I thinking about Denise? Had I wished that they leave me to myself, had I wished, to the contrary, that others gather round me? I found myself in a room I had never entered before. Every one of the things I had done in my life seemed to me unworthy of Denise. I slipped away without anyone noticing. Was it not extraordinary that I be able to do it such a short time after having been the object of so much attention? I headed for the forest as I had ten years earlier after having spent the night with Denise. I was surprised to be walking, to be wearing clothes. My life as of now had no further aim. So many important events had come to pass, had kept me occupied, and of them no trace remained. But a day is a long time. I distanced myself from my pain by dint of thinking. I wondered whether Denise had known that Colonel Laîsné knew me. I imagined that through generosity Richard had kept still. A secret between men. No, Denise had not known. She would never know, unless, once dead, you know all there is to know about the living. In this case, she knew many other things too.

Night was falling, the darkness made me afraid. I was unable to remain alone any longer. I retraced my steps. I walked up and down in front of the gate. Lights were visible through the slits of the metal shutters. Cars were parked in the garden. I did not dare go inside. I felt I had become a stranger. I thought about Denise. If she could see me, how she would understand my diffidence! I could hear her saying to me (she had said it to me so many times), "For heaven's sake, Jean, come inside." And I started to cry again.

The initial hours of immobility had passed. Denise was at rest. Her family hung about her, and as for me, I had abandoned her, I had been coward enough to wish that everything might end as quickly as possible, in order that I be spared the other sufferings, the formalities, the removal of the body.

One whole day spent in wandering had left such marks on my face that I could feel them. I felt the hollowness of my cheeks, the protrusion of my nose, the circles under my eyes, the creases of my wrinkles. Richard understood my distress, his family did too. However, they exchanged knowing glances. They did not blame my grief for being conspicuous, but for existing and for being sincere. That was more than they could stand. In their view, suffering was a further way of seducing. In this instance I was not an actor, that would be too vulgar, but a man who, because he lived intensely, had always succeeded in shuffling his sorry condition off into the background.

Towards ten o'clock I no longer had the strength to remain in that house. I should not have kept silent but spoken in a whisper like everyone else. I should have sought comfort among those presumably suffering as much as I. I had not been up to it. I had been thinking how I would never go back up to my room again. I was unable to leave. We do not spend years using certain objects without their finally having the look of belonging to us. I did not want to take any of them away with me, neither my brief case, nor the ashtray in Bohemian crystal Denise had given me, nor my tortoise shell combs and brushes, nor the accessories I had on my desk, nor my cuff links. I wanted nothing. The taking of any one object would have given me the temptation to take others. I wanted nothing, nothing, not even a handkerchief, not even a tie. Nothing, absolutely nothing. Yet I could not make up my mind to leave. In the end I went up to the third floor. My bedroom door stood facing me. Once I opened it, would I do the opposite of what I had decided? In the past, I would not have hesitated. I would have told myself that to go back on a decision was of no importance. I would have acted without regard for my original will. This time it did not happen that way. I went back down without having touched the doorknob. At last I perceived the light that is diffused in us by the feeling of having performed a fine deed. I was going to return to Paris, not only without taking anything with me, but without changing what I had been wearing.

I headed toward the station. Never in my life had I felt so strong. A fine rain sprinkled my clothes. So as not to run into anyone I took a roundabout way. Denise had not yet left the closed room where she lay. Yet leave it she must. No plea on earth could keep her there, and I did not wait until she was gone. The automobiles, all their lights turned off, stood in a row before the front steps, so spaced as not to impede each other. Slivers of light were coming through the joints between windows. And I was running away. I imagined the family, stupefied at first, then triumphant when they realized what I had done. I sensed that there were elementary rules that I was not abiding by. But it was too late, today, for me to turn into a man like the others. However, God knew how I abhorred making myself conspicuous, the efforts I had made to merit the consideration of my fellows. I had done a good deal of thinking in the course of recent weeks. I had tried to understand in what way I had sinned in order to be so unhappy. The world was having its way with me. I was beginning to hold a place in society. It was far indeed from resembling the one I had dreamt of! Be that as it may, I had become, it seems, a definable man. I had had the misfortune to be born under an unlucky star. I had not had a good upbringing. But I had married and, thanks to my wife's salutary influence, I had finally understood that if I did not aim at winning any special esteem, if I contented myself with my lot, I could occupy an honorable rank in the world. But Denise had died. I yet see her face on which life, as it withdrew, had left a mute understanding, a deep understanding of all the things human beings do. Would she reproach me at present for so lightly renouncing this honorable rank? As if there were someone forever stationed behind me to ascertain that I was playing a role, that I had never loved anyone, that it was self-interest that had dictated everything I had done, I murmured: "O Denise!"

I lay stretched out on my back, fully clothed. The corners of my eyes were moist as though I had just been reading. I got up for I had to walk. I felt about to break into tears. I flung myself back on the bed I had just risen from in order to hide my face. I was idling my time away, I was living and Denise was dead. All at once I turned over. This room—I was not acquainted with it. How had I been able to do so many things, to know so many people, and to be, today, so alone! I had left the light on when I got into bed. I fell asleep. Then dawn awoke me like broad daylight. Night had faded away without rendering me different. I went out a little later. I had not washed, done anything. I was still in the same shirt. It was seven in the morning. Was it that I wanted to be able to be present at the burial if the desire came over me suddenly? When an event in which we do not want to participate is imminent, should we proceed in such a way that it transpires without our noticing, or should we revise our attitude? I thought about Richard. Had he just lost his wife, oh! he would not be asking himself such a question! He loved his wife. They were an exemplary couple. Authority, work on the husband's part; affection, fidelity on the wife's. But why would the grief he felt be true, human, measured, whereas mine was turning into panic?

I was now walking more slowly. I had gone up to the Etoile. I was coming back down the Champs-Elysées. "To the Bois de Boulogne. To the Gare de Lyon," I used to say to the taxi driver when we wanted to be alone, Denise and I. I had just said to myself: "To Concorde." The streets were full of life. But there already was place de la Concorde. I headed into the little streets behind the Chambre des Députés. This time I forgot to set myself a destination. I was thinking of all the good Denise had done for me. How consoling it would have been had she not had only my interest in mind! I remembered those stormy days when I had seemed not to exist. Denise had been fighting for her happiness, and I experienced the delightful feeling of not being the sole cause of this struggle. I left all the struggling up to her, and it never entered her head to reproach me for this. She found it natural that the difficult tasks fall to her. I now wondered whether, deep down inside her, she had not been waiting for me to show more heart. I had believed that my inertia went unnoticed. I was no longer so sure of it. While walking along, I told myself that I ought to have spoken up, guided her, prevented her from doing certain things, instead of going into hiding, passing for weaker and more irresponsible than I was. People's attitudes, their remarks, their antipathy were becoming clearer. They were right. But how had they been able to ask a man like me to know that there are circumstances in which you must not just lie back and let yourself be loved?

Four days had gone by. The little money I had had on me was spent. It really required that I have no other choice for me to return to our little bank on rue Cambon, a street which leads, precisely, into boulevard de la Madeleine. Oh that quarter, how I hated it! It was the one where Richard and I had had lunch with an appraiser, where Denise's friends had their offices, where I had been out on the prowl during the war, because it was then the center of Paris, because a so very special odor having nothing of the odor of cooking used to come from restaurants, because I admired the tailors, the shirtmakers, the cafés, because, listening to the waltzes the public phonographs were playing, I would think back with nostalgia to a brilliant past that I however had never known. I was young and I was weeping for a bygone era!

And there I stood once again on rue Cambon. I recalled a day when I had been waiting for Denise. She had gone to the bank with her brother. He did not know that she was to rejoin me. To kill time I was walking up and down boulevard de la Madeleine. Suddenly I beheld brother and sister heading my way. What should I do? Cross the street? Simulate a chance encounter? But Denise called out to me. "We were looking for you everywhere," she said. "Where in the world were you?" She was not embarrassed. Richard had not shown the least surprise, but I had turned crimson with shame.

A third time I got to where the bank stood, identified on the outside by no sign or plaque. I made up my mind to enter. How much cash remained in our account? Denise had insisted that her account be in my name as well. "A joint account," the banker had observed. But legally, now that she was dead, did I have the right to withdraw the money in it? I did not pause to inquire. I would find out soon enough. I had lost all vanity. The thought that they perhaps did not know that Denise was dead was able to enter my mind without revolting me. I knew that it was for the last time I was standing in this bank. I loathed the place. I remembered those waits in the lounge when, without a penny to our names, we had asked for an advance against some unquoted stocks. Granting it to us, the director, René Poiret, had acted without due thought. However, he had later asked us to stop in. When we did he announced that to his great regret it was materially impossible for him to allow us this advance, since the stocks we had given him as security were not quoted. "You knew that!"

"Yes, quite, but in my mind we were dealing with the 1924 issue." I remembered the painful scene that had bro-

ken out a little while later on this very same rue Cambon.
How naive Denise had been! She had sought to persuade
me that if I went back to see René Poiret by myself, he
would not dare to refuse me this advance *because I was a
man*! He had refused only because she, Denise, had been
present. Now wasn't that adorable? For Denise I was a man
like other men. Neither my birth nor my behavior had
made her change her opinion. And I had yielded. I had gone
back the next day to see René Poiret. I was ushered into his
office just as he was on his way out the door to the Stock
Exchange. "Come back at five o'clock," he had told me. He
pretended, out of friendship for Denise, whom he had once
courted, not to see the eccentric side to her marriage and to
treat me like his other clients. I had returned at five. "So
very, very sorry, but as I told Denise in front of you, I
cannot allow you this advance." Amiableness had led him
so far as to say that he had done some inquiring that afternoon. I had persisted. I had appealed to his friendship for
us, even to his kindheartedness, so strongly aware was I of
Denise's desire that I succeed. I was so ill-acquainted with
men that, because he had listened to me politely, I thought
I had swayed him. And then all at once he had interrupted
me with this sentence which, simple though it was,
seemed to me to be coming from another world: "You
should disoblige me were you to press the matter any further."

My abrupt departure from Compiègne, instead of revealing
the deranged state I was in, could have been taken for indifference. I now did not care in the least. I was determined
never again to have anything at all to do with Richard. He
did not know where I was. I had gone off without leaving an
address as though he had not counted for anything better
than a vulgar innkeeper. I admitted that he had always

been in the right, and I, always in the wrong, without for all
that sensing any feeling of inferiority with regard to him. I
did write to him, however. There are certain satisfactions
we do not have the strength to deny ourselves. I wrote him
that I renounced the will Denise had made in my favor, and
asked him to burn it. For this there was no need. Richard
had certainly done so already, but I was set on his knowing
that my disinterestedness was conscious. In former times I
would have been loath to act in such a manner. Today kid
gloves were no longer in order. I needed simply to act as he
himself did, and whenever anything I did might win me
some consideration, not to scruple over publicizing it.
Since I had no idea then that I would be spending four years
in the rue Casimir Delavigne hotel where I had just taken
a room, I suggested (without bothering myself about the
conclusions he might draw) should he chance to have
something to communicate to me, that he write to me at
the rue Cujas poste restante.

To shut oneself up between four walls when one is suffering is a kind of mortification. I did not leave my room
except at mealtime. It seemed to me that in this way all the
harm I might have done Denise was atoned for. I remained
all day long sitting in front of the window, without newspapers, without books. Thus did two weeks go by. Denise
had been dead for seventeen days. Seventeen days!

I could no longer bear being cloistered this way. But before resuming my life I felt ever more strongly that I was
duty-bound to visit Denise's grave. The strangest ideas
were crossing my mind. That visit had to be made secretly,
no one in Compiègne must know. It would be comforting,
at such a moment, to have a friend who would give me
warm assistance, who would escort me, buy the railway
the tickets, who would look after me as one does a child.

One of the greatest disadvantages of isolation, is it not to be obliged to do everything onself? I remembered the privileged people I had known who were spared from everything. I recalled Madame Dechatellux's death. Neither Jules, nor Richard, nor the foregathered relatives had been distracted from their sorrow. By contrast I had to take care of my body and its needs. Once upon a time I had done this, joyfully, when having returned to civilian life I had to do my sewing, my washing, my cooking. Back then it had not occurred to me to envy those who were shielded from such chores. I had even looked down upon those spoiled children.

So I would go to Compiègne by myself. Having to attend to the material details of living is an excellent discipline, in times of happiness or in times of sadness. Nobody would accompany me. I was sorry about this, for in such circumstances friendships come forth strengthened. But just when my plan was giving me an objective once again I made a painful discovery. How had it happened that at the very moment I had the pious thought of going to kneel beside Denise's grave, I realized that I did not know where her grave was, that at the very moment I was preparing to act like other men, an unexpected detail showed me that I was still outside the human community? A year earlier, supposing I had found myself in a similar situation, I would have justified myself by invoking my special situation. But today what excuse could I plead?

Even so I went to Compiègne. I took the earliest morning train to avoid running into anyone when I arrived. "Why am I hiding?" I asked myself as I rode through the bright, deserted countryside. The sun, which had just come up, was already dazzling. Everyone was still asleep. The sun was shining for me alone. It must yet go on for a long space in solitude. Then clouds would hide it from mankind, when mankind awoke. What an intoxicating sensation of freedom I felt! Having lost everything, I had nothing left to lose.

No automobile was waiting at the level crossing in Compiègne. I was making an excursion into the past, but the time which had seemed so long since Denise's death was but a day when I crossed place de la Gare. My uplifted state faded away. I had pictured myself kneeling by a grave and I was calm. Even now was I giving way to Denise? She had thought, she had acted, and I had held my peace. I was still holding my peace. I remained immobile and mute as I had been during the big scenes, when she was alive.

I made off. I realized that this pilgrimage did not correspond to a need that sprang from my heart, that I had done nothing but conform to a custom. I discovered that the howsoever natural gesture of laying a flower upon a grave was not permitted to me.

What then was my purpose in going every day to rue Cujas? Richard and I, were we not strangers to one another? What could we say to each other now that Denise was no more? Did I need a sign of life in the solitude that surrounded me? Did the need for such a sign cause me to forget our mutual lack of understanding? Was I then continuing to acting within obscurity in a way I had not acted in broad daylight? Was it because nobody could see me that I was going to rue Cujas every day?

I sat down at an outdoor café on the Boulevard Saint-Michel. After all, wasn't I a man like the rest? Students went by, singing, jostling each other. I watched them. Their insouciance brought me relief.

TODAY

Hôtel Maillot, a Monday morning in January 1939. Twenty-one months have gone by since my so memorable meeting with Maître Logelin. I went back to see him four months ago. He had no sum at all to hand over to me. I asked him to inform Richard of my visit. Forty-eight hours later I received a check for eighteen thousand francs. My life, essentially, has not changed. The same alternation of ups and downs continues. I am happy, as I have often been when, after a difficult period, I found myself free from worries about tomorrow.

From my window I can see porte Maillot, the "Big Dipper" roller coaster, the moon over the Luna Park entrance, the white stripes on the pavement at this intersection with all its intricate road-signs. A light mist is floating above the first patches of new grass. The weather was lovely on Sunday. And smoke rises softly from the cast-iron incinerators where waste paper is burning.

I have arranged, despite its not being the practice in this hotel, to pay by the month. I was granted a ridiculously small reduction. Multiplying thirty-five francs (the price of my room by the day) by thirty (the average number of days in a month) you get one thousand fifty francs, and they dropped the fifty francs. In the old days I would unfailingly have refused a reduction whose insignificance did not off-set the advantage of paying the way everyone else does. But I accepted it, for I no longer care about the esteem I once thought I inspired by appearing to disdain personal advantages.

The tedious part of my dressing is finished. What remains can be protracted indefinitely. This includes picking out a shirt, a tie, the contemplation, which I do not like to hurry, of my overall person. It is not as vain as it sounds. When life smiles on us, we take pleasure, each morning, in restoring the previous days's bloom to our physical appearance.

Every so often I turn back to the window, as you do on a train when the landscapes change. Sparrows, which take flight only on big occasions, hop along my strip of outdoor ledge. I watch them peck at the crumbs fallen from the floors above. Do they see through glass?

Finally, I have a last look at myself in the mirror. No hint anywhere of faulty taste, of negligence. I am at my maximum. The thing now is to appear not to know it.

Today, I prefer to turn to the right, to walk up avenue de la Grande Armée. Another new day, more clouds, more sunshine. I went back to see Maître Logelin. Let us imagine that this fact become known to the entire world. Some would despise me. But would I not have the approval of others?

Reaching rue Duret, I come upon a former Spahi officer, Captain Lamoure. I see him here and there in Paris. We stop. The passers-by continue on their way. As for us, we are acquaintances.

"Come and see me," he tells me.

It has been such a long day that I arrive at the restaurant at six-thirty. I feel an urge to talk, to laugh, to be seen in a good humor. Without having done anything to bring this about, I sense that I am credited with a higher social standing than the other customers, that I would be viewed, if I were twenty years old, as a young man from a good family. They have not yet turned the lights on. I head toward the back. The owner, his wife, and the waitress are seated around a table. A young woman, the owners' daughter, is showing the things she bought this afternoon: silk stockings, a bottle of perfume, a box of stationery. All these objects are passed from hand to hand. And now I make an extraordinary observation. I too could take these objects being held out to me like snapshots in which I don't appear but which it would be unfriendly not to show to me. They are waiting for some sign of interest on my part. I do not move. I cannot touch those objects. They do not belong to me.

What happens next is stranger still.

"What do you think of this writing paper, Monsieur Jean?" the young woman asks me. "I bought it for my daughter. She doesn't want to write on anything but her own personal writing paper."

"She'll be pleased."

"But is it true that the writing paper they carry at Prix Unique comes from Japan?"

"I don't know."

" 'Made in Japan.' Here. Read what it says."

She holds out the box. I take it. But I came near to not taking it. In order to reach my hand forward I had to picture the general bewilderment a refusal would have caused.

It is four o'clock in the morning. I am in bed, stretched on my back. This is the position I prefer to smoke in. I like how my cigarette tastes when it has trouble remaining lit. I think about the man in the bunk next to mine, in a barracks, who also used to smoke at night. I am unable to get back to sleep, but no gloomy thoughts are haunting me. Yesterday I let myself go, physically as well as emotionally. Inside, I already feel what you would call a need to make up for that lost time.

"You're an early bird!" Henry Lamoure tells me when I show up at his office.

An officer at Compiègne, Henry Lamoure had known Denise, her parents, her uncle, Jacqueline, Madame Mobecourt and her sister, probably Colonel Laîsné as well, and everyone in the town's society. Naturally he had noticed that my presence there was tolerated and no more. He had nevertheless feigned unawareness of this. Made assistant director of the insurance company where Richard had thought of getting me a position, he had returned to Compiègne regularly, drawn by the hunting, the sports, the fairs, and not by dark family histories knowledge of which might have closed certain doors to him. Oh those festivals, those fetes in the park! How miserable they seemed to me, those paper lanterns they used for lighting, hung from wires stretched between trees! I did not realize that just as a stick is enough to make a puppet into a policeman, those lamps were enough to create the illusion of a night-time fete.

I have come to ask Lamoure to talk to me about Compiègne, to tell me the latest gossip. He announces to me that I am just the man he is looking for. He had brought up my name with the management, a conversation held by professionals about an amateur who may be useful. "Oh! don't get the idea that we'll treat you like a beginner. The commission you'll be receiving will be bigger than what our most senior people get. We want to strike out into new territory. We want to put together a team made up exclusively of men with connections and belonging to the same

circles. If, for example, you induce your Dechatellux uncle
to sign a contract with us. . . But do take a seat."

He hands me papers which he takes from various piles,
as they do in travel agencies. He is out of a certain schedule
of figures, he will mail me a copy.

"Study the whole thing. You'll let me know your answer. I repeat that this will be very much worth your
while."

Once out the door, I threw the papers away. Then I followed a pretty woman, without result. This led me down a
little street that ended in the Marché Saint-Honoré, where
I had never been. I waited for more than an hour in front of
the house she had entered. I ate lunch while reading a
newspaper. I had my coffee at Maison du Brésil on rue
Auber.

It is four o'clock by the time I get back. I open the window. It is a fine day. The sun is setting behind the Bois. It
has already sunk out of sight, but by hurrying up to the
hotel terrace roof I shall perhaps still be able to see it. It's
the lamp being taken away into an adjoining room. It lights
Saint-Cloud, and back here everything seems abandoned.
Dear God, I beg you, give me some purpose in life, let me
devote my strength to some noble and useful cause.

We are walking down the Champs-Elysées together. It is
eleven in the morning. The white roofs of the buses flow
along in the distance. The Tuileries are veiled in a gauze. Is
it dust or a country mist? It is pierced every now and then
by a gleam of light reflected from windows on rue de Rivoli.
We speak very little. It does seem that we have no reason
to stay together, and yet we stay. One evening, by chance,
Madame Vallosier entered the restaurant. She sat down at
the nearest table. She asked me to pass her the menu. Without reading it, she told the waitress: "Give me whatever

you have." She intrigued the customary diners. "Try to
find out who that lady is," the owner's wife whispered into
my ear.

We reach place de la Concorde. "Where do you wish to
go?" I really look as though I had no wish at all. "Should we
go to the boulevards and have an apéritif?"

Now I talk about myself. My father was an officer. But I
never knew him. My mother was a woman without means.
Madame Mobecourt, a lady in Compiègne who had taken an
interest in her, did nothing to marry her off. At present my
mother lives on rue Théodore de Banville. Anyhow, I was
consequently shipped from one place to another. I was a student at Lakanal, at a private school in Menton, at the lycée
in Nice. The war interrupted all that. Once discharged, I
wanted to rely upon myself alone, to be independent. I went
back to school, but I felt pressed for time. I lived through a
difficult period. It would make a surprising story. Then,
when I had understood that it would be impossible for me to
achieve what I desired, I returned to Compiègne and I married a childhood friend. But she died just as we were about
to settle ourselves in the south of France. I live alone at
present. I am still undecided on my next step.

I could keep on talking like this for hours, without con-
tradicting myself once.

I am off to see my mother. Now that nothing attaches me
to the past anymore, now that I am free of all outside influence, I no longer hesitate to visit those to whom I am
near, or who have drawn near to me. My mother left rue
Théodore de Banville years ago. She lives in a narrow, flat-
roofed house squeezed between two handsome apartment
buildings on rue des Acacias. The ups and downs the elderly go through always surprise me. I am too quick to
believe that the game is over with.

I climb a dirty stairway. I pull a bell cord and find myself face to face with my mother. She must now be in her sixties. I listen impassively as I am told that she is living with a son she had by one of her lovers. He is now twenty years old and studying medicine. For a long time the boy's father helped my mother out, but he does not give her any more money now. She explains that it was not for ordinary economy's sake that he stopped paying her anything. It seems that he has millions. She says they were not in agreement over how their son André should be educated. She at once adds that she continues to be on good terms with this man, has not kept up a grudge against him, does not think less highly of him. I sense that she is sincere. After having been so open with me, why has she to stiffen when I speak to her of how useful it would be for André to meet Richard, who is a doctor? She shifts the conversation. She informs me that she has just moved, that the building she left was still shabbier than this one. "It was an excellent occasion," I observed, "to ask André's father for some money." She explains that she did not do it lest this man (for whom I am beginning to have a decided dislike) imagine that she was counting on their relations in order to call on him at a later time. She hastens to add that he would not have refused her. But it comes to me all of a sudden that this man, about whom she has been going on with such satisfaction, long ago disappeared from her life. Mentioning him was a way of diverting my attention, of hiding a secret ambition from me. This ambition is that André become a great doctor. As well as rich, educated, and honored he will at the same time be grateful. When in your later years you have found a cause that deserves your single-minded dedication, you do not want to share with anyone the joy of seeing it triumph. A concrete goal replaces the vague happiness that you have been content to seek all your life. You accept neither advice nor encouragement. Others do not have the same reasons for desiring to achieve it that we do. However it be sincere, their approval by modifying in the face of the first obstacle may cast us back into the uncertainties of the past. My mother discovered that you must be strong to succeed. Her son will be strong. Her son will steel his heart for come what may. I look at him. How far he is from suspecting what is expected of him!

I go away, disappointed. The whole while my mother confided in me she was holding me at arm's length. For me it had been very disagreeable. I do not want to involve myself in her personal affairs. My past indifference forbids it, moreover. I think about André. We exchanged perhaps three words. He resembles me physically. I have an older brother's sense of superiority. Oh! I was careful not to let it appear. I believe now that my efforts were to little purpose for there is no doubt about it, André, in my mother's view, is her only son.

Though I have eaten nothing since morning (fixed meal-times, what has become of you!), I am neither hungry nor thirsty. I feel a kind of pressure in my temples, something like a pain which is unwilling to declare itself. And when I touch my fingers to them, this sensation disappears. It is a beautiful day. I look at the sun. I am able to maintain my stare for a second, focussing upon a point in its center that is less blinding than the fire it gives off. And this surprises me. The crowd is an unending succession of new faces without there being one that is known to me and without the whole striking me as unfamiliar. Life is an admirable thing, that is what I think. The distant memories whose happiness oppresses me . . . it seems to me that I am going to relive them in the future.

At a sidewalk café I sit down at one of the outermost

tables, from a sudden urge to make myself conspicuous. I rub my hands together with extraordinary rapidity, as though this gesture had some immediate utility. I feel strong enough to break something. I am seething. I am ready to explode. I point to a newspaper leaning a little too far out of a pocket.

"Your newspaper is going to fall, Monsieur."

I intervene in this wise more and more frequently. I clamp my jaws together. I don't need anybody. I ask nothing from anyone. I simply am. Consequently I have the right to contract my features, to challenge people, to strike my heels against the pavement.

"Monsieur!"

A fat man turns around.

"Beg your pardon. I beg your pardon, you resemble a friend of mine."

This time I clench my fists. I am trembling in a way that is altogether different from the trembling prompted by fear, by anxiety, by nervousness. I am trembling from strength. I am trembling like a fencing-foil. The future remains dazzling before my eyes. It is a way of being happy. I catch a confused glimpse of a time when all my dreams will be fulfilled, and I am transported with joy.

The weeding out has begun. No longer shall I preserve, deep within me, an unwarranted tenderness for Madame Mobecourt's sister. It is years since I last had a glimpse of her, and yet I went on imagining that we were connected by some secret link. Every time I took a decision I would ask myself what that woman would have recommended. What a strange thing it is, this belief that we inspire a special feeling in someone who knew us as children, this need we have to preserve, against who knows what calamity, an ultimate protection! Those calamities occurred, but

[141]

to me they never appeared great enough to turn toward that protection. And today, though nothing grave has occurred, I am taking the train to Versailles.

An old, undistinguished building, ill-situated since it is on a narrow street where the tram hugs the sidewalks and then waits, before proceeding, until the other tram has got through the switch. But in all that has to do with wealth I place no faith in appearances. For all its decrepit look, certain signs tell me that the people inhabiting the building are rich. The wide open doorway lends a ceremonial air to the dark vaulted passage within. The latter opens into a broad courtyard. Half the trellises upon which ivy must have climbed have been torn out. How that was done is something to see. The trellises were torn out cleanly, as they say, with no bits of lath left dangling, and the pieces that remain look like precious fragments. This courtyard is completely empty. No bucket anywhere about, no broom, no crate. I sense that for the inhabitants this emptiness is of value in itself, a luxury, something like the desire, from the entranceway on in, to afford no purchase whatever to malevolence.

I hide my agitation. It is instinct that commands me to show no emotion. To keep what you possess, you must begin by appearing unafraid of losing it. I climb the wide polished marble stairway. But I suddenly perceive that my self-assurance may proclaim the feeling that the barrier between us has fallen, that the years have brought us closer together, and that my natural character suffices to make up for that which is lacking to me. I have arrived. I do not want to ring. But I am too close to the bell to adjust to the idea of a trip made for nothing. I raise my hand. I bring my finger near the button of white bone right in the center of a circle of brass. I do not ring the bell.

*   *   *

At seven o'clock I am to meet Lucette, a clerk at Métyl's, by the Etoile metro station. She is keen on these meetings in the midst of a crowd. Each time I wonder whether she is going to turn up. You really have to want to get together in order to peer at every face coming up out of the metro. Is it because Denise hated this sort of rendezvous that I accept them with Lucette? I wait. People swirl around me. This is the shining hour for those who are at loose ends. It is the hour that makes all the others look dull, the hour for which certain people live. I remember a woman who used to sleep during the day, but who would not have missed being up and out at seven o'clock. I remember wanting to imitate her, to organize my life in such a way that it would not start until seven o'clock. Newspapers are being hawked beside me. The buses are full, and their bells ring merrily several times in a row. A constant circle of automobiles moves around the Arc de Triomphe. And here is Lucette. She is only a step or two away but she does not see me. I call to her just as she is about to move off. Oh, she would have come back, but I had a moment of fear. I look her over from head to toe. Not a word until I have done that. She is pretty. Upon her lips she has painted other, thicker ones. I think about all those people who called me a false friend.

Together we walk down avenue Wagram. I slip behind her to the other side so as to leave her on the left, for she is looking at the movie theaters. Behind her: that's what I said. Having reached the bottom of the sloping part of the avenue, we turn toward porte des Ternes in order to stay with the crowd. That morning I received a registered letter from a dentist concerning work done five years ago. I flew into a temper. How can a reasonable man neglect his debts? Were Denise there, we could have talked of that letter. What can I tell Lucette about it? She would advise me to pay a first installment, or not to answer. But she would not tell me what I desire to hear.

We stop to read a restaurant menu. Then we continue along. At nine o'clock we go to a movie. At midnight, without much conviction, I try and talk Lucette into staying. I know that she cannot, that her parents are expecting her. She leaves me.

Now I am alone. I am unable to return to my room. I am looking for an adventure: a woman in the grip of erotic frenzy, having left her place of residence in order to give herself to the first man she sets eyes on. I dream of being that man, I dream that there be no choice, that it truly be because I am the first man she happens upon.

I walk down avenue Foch, but when I reach porte Dauphine I retreat despite the temptation to keep on. I am afraid of the Bois de Boulogne. Even in the worst moments I remain prudent. Some reassuring professionals accost me. I fend them off politely, giving them to understand that I look upon them as human beings. I must not be the only one to show them such consideration for they express no gratitude at all. When Denise was alive, I so arranged things that I was never in this plight, on my own for a whole evening. But, at present, I am on my own every evening.

A white light illuminates the Arc de Triomphe. Without knowing how, I end up at the point I started from. To be so without anything to do! To have walked so far just to wind up back at the Etoile metro station! For a few minutes I pretend to be waiting for someone. Then I head off again along avenue Foch. The women must recognize me because, depending on the idea they have of me, they either ignore me or have at me more persistently. I turn and start back. I cannot keep on walking any longer. My shoulders hurt and, as always, I think it's the weight of my overcoat. I have a longing to take a bath, to read a newspaper that may have just begun publication. How I would love to have a mother, a sister, a wife waiting for me! They would ask me questions. They would wonder what could have kept me. No more unavowable desires. But nobody is waiting for me and I am incapable of returning to my room. I know I shall return only when it has become very late, once I have realized that the streets are as empty as my room.

I recross all the spokes of the Etoile. Now I am back standing in front of the grim metro station. The steel grill at the bottom of the stairs is closed. It has something terrifying about it. I walk into a café and lean my elbows on the counter. A man is already there. He may be forty-five. Though he is not heavy, I notice that his abdomen sags a little. On the lapel of his threadbare overcoat are the ribbons corresponding to two military decorations. He fought in the war, he is now a petty official or a clerk. Such is the warmth I feel for this sort of man that I make his acquaintance. How close I feel to him and, at the same time, how far away! The war has been over for twenty years. For twenty years he has been freely moving about in Paris, and yet nothing in his life is not familiar to me. I did not fight in the war, to his mind I am still wet behind the ears, and yet he is not interested in having an edge over me. There is the man I should have been in order to talk to Richard, I should have been the glorious captain wearing the Legion of Honor, the Military Medal and a Military Cross with three palms, who would dine with his general in Paris, who, once discharged, became president of the 153rd's chapter of the Veterans' Association.

We go on talking. I ask him whether he got up to Verdun. He tells me a few stories. He has seen that I was a soldier. At no time does he question me. Oh, the admirable discretion of those who have been to war! He has himself another brandy. This is the third glass he has drunk while I am there. How I wish I had the right to live this openly! How I wish the influence of the war upon my life were more evident! How I wish my distress, instead of proceeding from such miserable causes, were that of all the men of my generation! It is two o'clock in the morning. As someone who has finished her work, a woman joins us at the counter. She listens to us, talks not about her brother but her father who was killed in 1916. For the first time, my companion has questions to ask. He wants to know where, in what regiment.

Soon there are only the two of us, she and I, and I abandon my restraint. The seriousness of our conversation had indeed held me back for a few moments. Then I smiled. That was all it took. She understood and asked me to follow her. We walked down rue Brey, we went into an hotel. Never would I have followed a woman but for this combination of circumstances. Going up the stairs, I try to explain to myself what has happened. Now I am about to be ridiculous with my fear of catching a disease. My companion is too prompt to understand my fear for me to have been the only man to experience it in her presence. This discovery of the points that we men have in common gives me an uneasy feeling. Then I realize that behind this woman's total obedience to my desires there lies a certain skill in guiding them toward a kind of love suiting to her. I am touched by this as though by a maternal attention. "Just make yourself comfortable, my little guy. I am going to get myself ready. Do you want me to pull the curtains?" Tomorrow, I think to myself, I shall be back again in the presence of children, of old people. Is there something in my intimate life that makes it worse than that of others?

"You're afraid I've got something? You can just set your mind at rest."

"It's hard to," I say, as if my business in life forbade me from putting myself at risk.

"I'm in good shape, I swear to you."

She is sincere. I feel she has a sense of professional responsibility. I visualize, in the event she were to infect me, all the trouble they will give her at police headquarters. Police headquarters! And now I visualize the boulevard Saint-Michel—I have forgotten all about the lady-friend of mine who lives there. I want to remain the serious gentleman, apprehensive, who is readying himself to rejoin his family.

The city is still as brightly lit as after dinner, but the streets are almost deserted. I am in an odd frame of mind. On the one hand I feel a deep disgust with myself for having lain with that woman, and on the other hand I know that I used discretion and that it is materially impossible that I be punished for it. So there is no element of fear in the uneasiness that grips me. Nevertheless, the girl may well have contaminated me simply by shaking hands with me, or by that very chaste kiss with which she had wished to express affection at the start, not knowing the sort of man she was dealing with. Then I find comfort in the thought that, come daylight, in a few hours' time, these fears shall vanish once and for all. Now that it's all over with, how pleased I am not to have given in! But I came very close to it. At a certain moment I had felt ashamed of my precautions. I had thought: "I'm acting like a little old timid soul." I almost clasped her in my arms.

I have both elbows resting upon the telephone book shelf in the booth. I am talking in a way that aims at pleasing. After that I walk back up into the open air. My adventure with Madame Vallosier strikes me as most mysterious. I can see her only on certain days, at certain hours. I have to seem as though I know where I am going when I pass in front of the concierges' wing. The concierges' wing! I had forgotten about that, too! A few years ago I would have been afraid of a scandal. But today it does not matter what happens.

I go up to Madame Vallosier's. Gone is the time when a simple rendezvous with a woman was enough to gladden a day. Madame Vallosier lives in an apartment in a group of buildings owned by a cooperative. The garden in the middle of the central courtyard, the wrought-iron gates, the spa-style lamp posts, give this little complex an air of luxuriousness. There is still something of the provincial in me and it allows me to imagine that one of these buildings contains Jules Dechatellux's bachelor's establishment of which I had heard so much. Perhaps I shall bump into him one day. I must confess that it would please me.

Her apartment looks out on the gardens of the Villa des Ternes. It is comfortable, tastefully furnished, and in it you don't so much sense the regard for money as in the homes in Compiègne. Here spending is done without much forethought.

Madame Vallosier likes me a whole lot. I felt that she thought me well brought up, that she secretly admired my manners, my sophisticated ease, my familiarity with conventions, which proves that you always have for somebody else those qualities that you suffer from not having. I have won her trust. If this woman were the only person I knew in the world, I might believe that there was no difference between Richard and myself.

On leaving her, something occurred to me and I was much struck by it. The present is a continual struggle. One cannot foresee how a new friendship will evolve. Newly-made acquaintances may turn into our enemies, whereas those whom we have neglected may love us. Of my old

friends I have none left. I suffer from being surrounded by
nothing but precarious friendships. Whenever I see the
clerk at Métyl's, I am happy, but will she not hate me
tomorrow?

I catch myself thinking longingly of Denise. I imagine our
life, our happiness if we were sharing the room in the Hôtel
Maillot. Now that she is dead, everything seems so easy to
me. Why were we so very concerned with family, with fortune, with self-esteem, when it would have been so simple
to love each other in peace and quiet at the Hôtel Maillot?
Why? So it is the same ignorance that has always kept me
from being happy! Just as I was once incapable of joining the
army, so, three years ago, I was not able to live with Denise
in a modest room. Life unfolds as if things were outside our
control and suddenly, when it is too late, we realize it would
have been easy to render it favorable to us.

I go back to my mother's. It has been freezing weather for
the past several days and the apartment, although barely
heated, feels warm. It is early, but even so my mother
already has her hat on. She does not want a cozy family
atmosphere around her. Not one cushion anywhere, not
one comfortable armchair. Everything is subordinate to her
son's success.

On my first visit I was received rather ceremoniously
and I entered no farther than the dining room. Now I go
into the other rooms. I am surprised by the disorder and the
dirt. Through an unclosed door I behold André pulling on
his clothes while seated on a folding cot whose sheets trail
upon the floor. A wooden box serves as his night table, for
his newspapers, and for something to put his feet on. Such
slovenliness is incomprehensible. Nothing can account for
it. It is not the result of carelessness or poverty. Rather it is
a kind of defying of the demands of everyday life. Lost in

her dream of the future, my mother refuses to see them. She struggled against them for years, and every time she saw them come back as numerous as before. She gave up the fight. Dirt no longer bothers her. She no longer feels the need to get rid of it because she knows that, tomorrow, she will have to begin anew. A far wiser course is to surrender the place to the enemy, accomodate yourself to him so as not to have to think about him anymore.

We chat in a bedroom that she has arranged for herself, but which is just as dirty as the other rooms, with the one difference that the furniture has been pushed to the farther end and that one corner of a table, where she in the habit of having her coffee, is covered with a napkin. Why is it that all the furniture is rickety, broken, that the upholstery is torn, stained? Nothing is clean, neither the writing paper nor the insides of the drawers, where you would think it had rained. They are full of crumbs, dust, dried mud from I don't know where. The bathroom is in the same condition. Entire clumps of bristles are missing from the toothbrushes. The glass, a piece of it gone from one side, can be filled only halfway. The rod running around the wooden shelf the wash-basin sits upon is dangling at one side. As for the bathtub, it is black. But what is inconceivable is that I feel no aversion for this interior, that foremost among my thoughts is the effect it would produce upon a Dechatellux. Actually, I don't feel all that uncomfortable here. I move around in all this easily enough. It even seems to me that if I had to live here, I would quickly feel at home. The gatekeepers' lodge looms out of the past. Behind it stands the woodcutter's shack. We have the same origins, my mother and I. We had forgotten them, she on her side, I on mine. One winter day our paths cross again. I realize that the life I have led far away from her does not prevent me from being her son.

I had supposed I was luckier than my mother, had advanced to the edges of a more sterling world than hers. I am of a mind to offer some advice. I let it be understood that even if a lofty ambition causes us to look disdainfully upon down to earth matters, we ought, if only for the sake of our loved ones, to hold to a minimum of decency. André is a good and sweet-tempered person. Perhaps it is hard on him to live in such uncomfortable surroundings.

My mother does not seem to understand what authorizes me to speak to her this way. She has always looked with distrust upon the class of people I lived amidst. Listening to me it is as though they were talking. She changes the conversation. But you are always misconstruing people. I had believed that my mother resented me for having grown up where she had been so badly treated. I had believed she was strong, and now I suddenly realize that she fears me. She fears lest my counsels have more influence upon André than her own. She fears subtleties. She fears that André will let himself be seduced, that he will get the idea there are other means to succeed besides work. Work however is the only means she is sure of, and from it you must not deviate under any pretext. She fears lest her son come under my sway, lest he change, lest he move away from her. She can retain her authority only by remaining intransigent. If she departs from her line of conduct, if she agrees to intriguings and recommendations, she knows she will become an obstacle to success instead of being its architect.

Seen in perspective, I recognize that there was not just disinterestedness in my love for Denise. Now that I am leading an independent life, that I am beholden to no one, the past is becoming clearer. The most insignificant incidents are the ones which open our eyes. Lucette's father wanted to meet me. He paid me a call. We had a chat together. Facing him, I had the feeling of being a man. Self-possessed, I alone was master of my words, of my actions. The unbounded exhilaration we feel when we are truly free! Whatever promise I made, I could keep it. Whatever I chose to hide, no one could disclose it. Altogether ordinary though that man was, I experienced a magnificent hour in his company. How had I managed for so long to put up with the tutelage of Denise? Had I not exaggerated to myself my love for her out of shame over my material dependence?

Have I a changeable character? Behold me today thinking of confiding in Madame Vallosier as though to a woman I were in love with! Behold me, realizing that I am alone, that I am in need of tenderness and, naturally, of protection! Behold me as I hesitate, not because I perceive the fancifulness of my intention, but because, as in the past, I fear lest my effusiveness today be to my detriment in the future! And behold me referring to a "future" for which I don't care a fig! And behold me now wanting to say to Madame Vallosier that I am unhappy, that I need to be loved, understood!

I sometimes ask myself whether I am not crazy. When I started out in life, my dream was to complicate things for myself in order to be able to find pride later on in the obstacles I had overcome. I trust that I am not about to go through that all over again today.

I have another half-brother, a shoemaker in Buttes-Chaumont. My mother has just informed me of this. Since I now go to see her from time to time, it is something I should know. This revelation has had a considerable impact upon me. Thus, at the very moment I have the desire to live an open life, one in which I would not mind taking along some such person as Richard on a visit to my mother,

I am told that I have a brother who makes shoes. I too easily imagine that I have got rid of pride. It is useful that a piece of news like this, by wounding me in my very depths, serve to show me that I am ever the same. "Marcel would like very much to get to know you," my mother told me. I went to see him. He is in his thirties. He talked to me. There were, I saw, a good many analogies in our two lives. Raised in a working-class suburb by an old woman, he had regarded his mother, whom he seldom saw, as a marvelous being. That was my story with Jacqueline. But he was less lucky than I. His mother came less and less often. He stayed on in his working-class neighborhood. He went through the local elementary school, was apprenticed. And he became a shoemaker. He introduces me to his wife, to his children. The eldest boy is already ten. He looks at me, his big blue eyes full of wonder. Am I in my turn a personage able to strike a young imagination? And the wife also looks at me wonderingly. So he's a relative, a brother of my husband and André! Proudly they show the shop to me, then the living quarters. They waited four years before they could rent it. Before, they lived a few houses away, in lodgings that were much smaller. "You see," my brother told me, "you should never lose hope."

I go on my way. Marcel and I know our mother, but neither he nor I knows our father. We are brothers. And yet how far apart we are! I cannot believe that the man I have just left has suffered as much as I have. But, after all, what do I know? Slowly I walk back down from Buttes-Chaumont. The sun is setting. The air is cold. I think that my difference from Marcel may possibly be very slight. Oh, how I wish Denise were here! Only a woman who loves us can say reassuring things to us at such times. "Why no, you have absolutely nothing in common," Denise would tell me. She would persuade me. She would prove it to me.

Everybody knew that my father was a man of the world. I had lived in an environment that could not be compared to the one Marcel had lived in. But Denise is no more. And after considering my life coolly, I feel that there is not so much difference between my brother and me.

Albeit off in a remote part of Paris, I do not look for a bus. I walk past the terminal from which buses go to Compiègne. No memory arises in my mind. I am sad. To have come all this way in order to wind up in front of this bus station! I am today nothing more than the man I would have been had nobody ever concerned himself with me, had I never met Denise, had I done as my mother had advised after my discharge and quietly found myself a niche in some branch of the administration (assuming they would have accepted me). As I was doing today, I would be returning from Buttes-Chaumont where I would have visited my brother. A place in society would belong to me. Like Marcel I would envy what my mother was doing for André.

I walk along boulevard de la Chapelle. I used to think that a familiarity with bourgeois life, its ways, its prejudices, was an acquisition. At present I doubt this. I lived only for the space of a twenty-day leave in this part of Paris. Yet memories spring up from all sides. Here I am on rue Pajol where I found a place to stay from midnight on, here is the big cinema which seemed so expensive. How it has aged! There is the café where I met a woman who gave me such an awful scare. I had left. I was unable to see her again. And she wrote to me from the hospital! Was I too going to fall ill? She was apologizing to me, I think. I am no longer able to remember. When memories are sharp, they already affect us emotionally. But when they are vague like this one, they can be overwhelming. At that time, Marcel was growing up in his working-class suburb. How far we were from each other! Today, for an outsider with an eye exclusively for the facts, we have been reunited.

I wend my way homeward. What a home! I would like to stop, rent a room in one of these streets that mount toward some side or other of Sacré-Coeur, and never show my face at my hotel again. Nobody is lying lifeless in my room. Just as I left Compiègne, so I would like to leave porte Maillot. But in the evening it is nice to go back to where there are people you know even if you do not care for them, to be greeted by someone, be it in an unfriendly manner, just so long as nobody looks up and asks who you are. I would have done it in former times. I would have walked into the first hotel I saw. Before stepping back out, I would have marked my place by leaving my overcoat behind, regardless of the cold weather, and I would have roamed around all evening, and all night too, in my search for a woman. The next morning, I would have gone to the public bath and waited for my evening date. And if no one turned up, I would have gone out looking again. And if my expeditions proved fruitless, I would have gone to bed so late that I would have fallen asleep at once. I felt pride in everything, in the simplest acts, like eating a sandwich at a café counter.

Brothers, my own as well as other people's, hold in my life an importance that surprises me. Now it turns out that Madame Vallosier has a brother. Why, I wonder, did she desire that I make his acquaintance? Is it to show she trusts me, or that in the event of danger she would not, like Germaine, be alone? Is she as fond of him as she says? She maintains that he is younger than she and that she has remained his big sister.

So I met this younger brother. After what I had heard about him, I was expecting to be introduced to a distinguished young man, considerate, discreet, admiring of his sister. He turns out to be a hulking big fellow who seems to do everything grudgingly, and whose elegance evokes that of a pimp. How can Madame Vallosier have failed to realize that such a brother is damaging to the idea she wishes to give of herself? How does she not see that he renders her quite as suspect as Marcel would render me suspect in her eyes were I to present Marcel to her? I shall answer these questions right away. He is her real brother. They grew up together under the same roof. He cannot make her ashamed of him, however unlike the paths they have chosen. True family spirit, is it not this acceptance of human beings such as they are, with all their defects, is it not this indifference about anything in them that could redound to our discredit?

Pale winter-time sunlight enters my room. From my bed I can see it settle over the roofs of buildings. A similar kind of sunlight accompanied me when I returned to Compiègne after Denise's death, when I started out on rue du Château-d'Eau for a stroll through the better parts of town.

I get out of bed. The day will be so long that I dawdle about while dressing. Shall I be, when lunch is over, the sort of customer who arrives with people who are in a hurry, who orders his coffee when they do, but who then rests his forearms on the table, pushes back his chair for room to cross his legs, and lingers after the others have gone?

The chambermaid brings me my breakfast, to which three pats of butter and a teaspoon of jam give a falsely copious air. She asks me when I plan on going out, for she wants to do the room. The previous evening has left me with such a feeling of disgust that I grope for some way of avoiding another like it. That is when the idea occurs to me of coming back to my room after lunch. It will be two o'clock. In my absence, a fire will have been lit in the fireplace. At four o'clock, tea and little cakes will be brought up to my room without my having to ring. In the evening I shall be brought something light, cold cuts. My shutters will be closed, the curtains drawn before nightfall. I shall have given the electric switch two turns to light the four bulbs of the overhead fixture. The bedside lamp will shed unnecessary light on my pillow. I try to interest the chambermaid in all these preparations by asking her for suggestions. I shall buy some newspapers, a deck of cards, maybe a book. I shall play a few hands of solitaire. It so happens that today is the day they iron the bed-linen downstairs. I shall leave my door ajar. The fact that I have been able to put so much intimacy into an afternoon at the hotel is a source of relief.

I take a short walk. The one objectionable thing is that the weather is good. But the finest winter day always turns gray after lunch.

Therefore I come back at two o'clock. Everything has been prepared as I had asked. A pleasant surprise awaits me. I am not the only one who has organized his time in his room. Another door is open. I see a big man in his shirt sleeves, sitting on the edge of his bed. He is watching the chambermaid close the shutters. Unlike myself, he has not given any instructions. He has made no arrangements at all. However he seems to have more solid reasons than I do for remaining in his room—correspondence, perhaps accounting to attend to. I hear him ask for ink, for paper, for another pen. Somewhat later, in a casual way, as though surprised that someone else has decided to stay indoors for the rest of the day, I say to the chambermaid: "He has the right idea. It's still when you are in your own place that you're best off."

I have so many hours ahead of me that I do not take off my overcoat right away, or close the door. I do not interrupt the chambermaid. I wait for her to finish with my neighbor. I am in no hurry at all. Every now and then I take a few steps down the hallway, then come back as if I had changed my mind. A little later I repeat the same thing. This is when I discover a detail that delights me no end. Even though their work is done, the employees are supposed to stay on, to keep busy. The door to the linen room stands open. A pile of sheets comes up in the elevator, which is against the rules. They are not immediately picked up and removed. The maids are having a chat. And even though it is daytime, all the lights are on.

Finally the moment comes when I cannot do otherwise than shut myself in my room. Among my morning purchases is a pair of red leather slippers which, by the way, were rather expensive. I have taken off my jacket, my vest, but kept on my collar and tie. I maintain appearances just for myself. Nothing can happen, but you never know. I sit down in an armchair, near the fireplace. The deck of cards, the book, the newspapers are within hand's reach. Now all that remains for me to do is not be bored. Yet I get up from time to time to shift the position of some object. Nothing must offend my eye. Above all I must postpone the moment when everything will be done.

Four o'clock strikes. My tea is brought to my room as I have ordered. But why are they using the same cups, the same jars of jam, the same tray they used this morning? This isn't tea, it is yet another breakfast. I feel a small satisfaction. It requires a certain refinement to notice such a detail.

"The same cup?" I ask the chambermaid, a faint irony in my voice.

She looks at me in surprise.

"Never mind, never mind," I conclude, in the manner of a man who knows that others are not going to understand him.

How ridiculous this is! Oh, how I wish I were somewhere else! But where? I get up to serve myself. The dangerous hour is now upon me. I fight the urge to open the curtain. In the end I cannot keep from doing it. Night has fallen and in the darkness the lights are shining. Daylight disappeared only a brief moment ago and they have a special freshness. Women stop in front of the tall window of a flower shop. Nowhere do flowers smell better than in Paris. I feel like going out. I gaze into the fireplace with the hope that the fire will detain me. Indeed I have just put on two new logs. They lie amid the flames without having yet begun to burn and I have got to go out.

It's Sunday. I am expected for lunch at Lucette's parents'. When she invited me, the look I had from her hinted that my acceptance caused her a pleasure that went beyond that of simply spending the day with me. As so many other people have done, she must have spoken about me in such a way as to imply that she stood nearer to those she was speaking to than to me. I accepted because I knew that I would be received with great kindness. I have never cooked or kept house, but I take a petty bourgeois pleasure in going to places where I won't have to lift a finger, where everything will be done for me. That is how it will be at the home of Lucette's parents. Having company, for those fine people, means sparing your guest even the trouble of shifting a chair.

The morning creeps slowly by, for nowadays I wake up early, at seven o'clock, at six, even at five. I know that they are glad to be having me, and my thoughts stray from this lunch.

At eleven o'clock, I take the stairs down. I have just walked out of room number thirty, like the thirty on my desk at the lycée. The staircase is padded in soft carpet. Now my thoughts are on this lunch. I do not enjoy the feeling that preparations are under way. I did not have my café au lait brought to my room, which was in order to save, I believe, seven francs. Let it be noted that I do not know what amount I have economized. I am generous. I spend without thinking, as they say. But I contracted habits in the wake of the Dechatelluxes. I learned, not to appreciate the value of money, but to keep an eye on doings likely to bring on expenditures. And of this habit I am still proud.

It is a gray Sunday. The deserted avenue has the look of a cordoned-off area an hour before the ceremony. Everything is ready. The officials are going to arrive. I stop and chat with the man you buy the tickets from. I like to joke with the persons who would not joke if I owed them something. Then I walk up to the Etoile, saving myself one fare. I feel none the worse for having gone without breakfast and a stretch on the bus, and in my pocket I have an extra eight francs, or thereabouts. If I don't watch out I may acquire a taste for these exercizes and come to resemble still further the overcautious mouse I picture in my imagination. I shall try to diminish myself, to shrink, instead of trying like everyone else, like Lucette, like Lucette's parents, to magnify, to enlarge myself.

I must buy a cake. I absolutely must. Nevertheless I hesitate. "At present I have the position of a man in life," I end up telling myself, "and I'll just do it, I'll buy a cake without thinking about it, because there isn't anything more natural." I shall arrive cake in hand. But shall I buy it at Boissier's, for instance, or around Barbès-Rochechouart? For several minutes I stew over the matter. I decide on Boissier's. I shall look as though it had never so much as crossed my mind to buy it elsewhere. It costs twenty francs instead of twelve. But everyone will taste the difference. They won't say anything, but they will recognize the value.

I spy my cake in a pastry shop on rue Rodier. But it is not the same. The decoration is less delicate. The swirls of cream suggest a peasant hand. Such are the differences to which I attach so much importance.

The rue Rodier I recall was a steeper street, more crowded with people, it had a more working-class feel. But climbs are becoming less sharp. During the war I took a walk up to Sacré-Coeur one day. I thought I was scaling a mountain. Nowadays it sits upon an inconsequential knoll.

Rue Rodier ascends hardly at all. I am beginning to think peculiar thoughts again. Being seen entering Lucette's building bothers me. Every door in Paris is the same to me. I enter anywhere. But not while cutting such a ridiculous figure: a cake in my hand, a closely-fitting overcoat, turned-down gloves, a felt hat with upturned brim placed squarely on my head, whereas in the past I wore it tilted back and to the side. Today my desire is to appear elegant.

I feel now like giving my cake to the first person who seems to me apt to accept it. This would be an original thing to do, one of those gestures to which I used to attribute an underlying meaning and which led me to part with far more precious objects.

"Monsieur, allow me to offer you this cake."

"Monsieur, I don't know what to make of this. I don't understand. I have no reason to go along with such a thing."

"Please accept it, Monsieur."

And now I am obliged to lie, lie to get someone to accept what I am giving away. Admirable, isn't it?

"I was expected for lunch at the home of some friends, I

wanted to bring them a cake. But they must have forgotten that I was to come for they're not at home."

In my voice, nothing whatever to indicate disappointment or hint at blame.

"In as much as I shall be having lunch at a restaurant, I don't want to look as though I were bringing my dessert."

I scan some passers-by. Not one strikes me as capable of accepting anything whatever from a stranger. In the end I step into the dark lobby of the building. A small windowed door gives access to the stairway. It is not the way it is in working-class buildings, where there are no such doors. I open it, and right there in front of me rises the stairway, whose first step, like the first rung of a ladder, is no wider than the rest. I climb up to the fifth floor just as Lucette told me. The farther up I go, the more cheerful everything seems to become. That's what happens in apartment buildings of this kind. The mediocrity fades as you get farther from the entrance. Something more and more personal emanates from more light-colored walls. At each new floor three fewer families go past on the landing. Eventually you remain alone with those you are visiting.

I pull the bell. I have difficulty pushing the brass plunger back in, coated as it is with dried oil. The door opens and Lucette greets me. She has no hat, no coat, no handbag, but she is still in the same dress. She is still the salesgirl at Metyl's. She was bright enough to understand that it is thus she looks her best, that as an alert salesgirl is how I prefer her. I present her with the cake. The cardboard box with its cleverly interlocking flaps, the little piece of wood whose notch keeps the string from slipping, the name Boissier printed everywhere, do definitely make more of an impression than wrapping paper tied up with a bow. I am shown in. It is a modest apartment, but everything is there. I recall seeing several of this type back in the days of Germaine. You can fairly hear the words: "We may not be rich, but we don't deprive ourselves of anything." I sense that these apartments are not as foreign to me as I would like to have it believed.

The conversation at table starts on a lively note. It seems that we are sorry we did not get to know one another sooner. Suddenly, at the end of the meal, I come to a strange realization. We have not said anything. Its preliminaries have been the conversation itself.

Not for an instant do Lucette's parents think of bringing it home to me that because of their daughter I have obligations towards them. It is a joy, for this little family, to have me here. They display an excessive consideration for me. They understand that Lucette and I would not have waited to be married before having intimate relations. I recall Lucette's comment: "You'll see, it isn't at all what you are thinking." She is quite right. But herein lies the tragedy. This broadmindedness does not render me better. Deep in my heart I remain contemptuous of this narrow life that could so easily have been mine. Lucette senses this and her face becomes sad. I talk with animation in order to appear touched by her parents' welcome. They are looking at me oddly now. Was it not presumptuous of me to come here? Had I not imagined that condescension could be concealed?

On saying goodbye I cannot resist the urge to display my effortless self-confidence. My departure is perfect. I seem to hear them saying: "He's a genuine man of the world." As I back my way out I do not trip over any furniture. I am so sure of myself that I even pause to move a chair aside so as to forestall an unpleasant incident for others.

I proceed toward the Châteaudun intersection. My head feels stuffy from alcohol. Gold from the invisible sun suffuses the mist. From out of the back-shops of the dealers in antiques, in old prints, in postage stamps comes an idea of the comfort of bourgeois apartments. My thoughts turn to the pleasures which correspond to the poetry of this waning winter afternoon. Loving, being loved, these are insufficient. One must love because one has done fine things. Pleasures must be linked, this joy must not be unique, there must be others, such as having friends and fortune.

I walk past the Opéra. I cannot prevent myself from turning down rue Cambon. There is the building. By day its shadow cuts across the narrow street, and by night, its glow. Today nobody walks up the stairs to the bank for me. "Go on up," I used to say to Denise, "I'll wait for you in this café." That café is still there, a café where they are careful with electricity, where the personnel of the neighboring hotels find a modesty reminiscent of their origins. Mixed in amongst the employees I would be on the lookout behind the curtains. I do not mix in with them anymore. Even so, I have not changed so very much. That lunch with Lucette and her parents proved it. How it dragged on! What an idea, to tell me about a purportedly very rich uncle who drives around in a car and owns a former monastery in the Gironde! I had an urge to say that I detested him. What a dropping of jaws! It would have been pointed out to me that I did not know him. I would have answered back that I despised him anyway. And a hush would have fallen upon the table overladen with food.

I am going to go back to my room. Being recognized by the manager, by the cashier, by the chambermaids nowadays leaves me indifferent. I know I shall not be able to prevent myself from going out again. So why even go back?

It is ten o'clock in the evening. I have just switched on the light and, for a few seconds, the room I see has the look of belonging to a stranger. I put away my clothes so that they will not be spoiled. There was a time when I would dream of tossing them here or there, when I marvelled at the off-hand manner in which certain women undress. I bring my trouser cuffs up to the light, those cuffs that have grazed the ground all day long. I shake out the insides where some bread-crumbs have lodged. I inspect my shoes. Everything is more rapid now, not only the wearing out of things, but the growth of nails and hair. I foresaw that someday I would be alone again and that I would then rid myself of the odd habits I had contracted during married life. That day did come, but I have just as many odd habits. I become even more attached to things. It distresses me that in our shared life they take so little account of the time I have yet to exist, that they are so quick to play me false. The conditions are there for me to change for the better. And an old habit has scarcely done fading away than a new one appears.

I stretch out on my back, arms above my head, savoring the coolness that enters the hollows of my armpits. I think: "Here is a man on his bed just like thousands of others." Am I going to lose myself in speculations of a general nature? No. I get up. In order to do something, I shake out my handkerchief in front of the fireplace. The chimney draft draws away a few specks of dust. A thread of water dribbles into the sink. I tighten the faucet. It does no good, the dribble continues. Its descent into the basin is noiseless, but I must tell the chambermaid. My head aches. Even so minute a detail gives me the impression that the whole world is against me.

At last, midnight strikes. I am going to be able to go to bed. The light once out, I do not fall asleep. I turn the lamp on, I get up. I like getting up, imagining that my bed is not a nest but a kind of couch. This is connected with my notions about freedom, about genuine comfort. I hate those carefully tucked in beds of people who are always cold. Space, a neat floor so that I can walk barefoot, a mild temperature, that is what I like. I have got into my pajamas. My underwear and shirt and socks are strewn over the chairs. In this little routine I play the part of the man who never thinks of hiding anything. This is the way I like being surprised in the morning, after saying "Come in!" to the chambermaid, then exaggerating the yawns and grimaces of awakening.

That chambermaid is a fat woman from Brittany. My coquetries with her are the more incomprehensible in as much as they vanish the moment I am dressed. The behavior I then affect with her is that of a generous master toward a poor servant. The other Sunday I gave her some rusks that had softened. Just yesterday I absolutely insisted that she take her husband a pair of shoes I had stopped wearing. "Starting tomorrow, I won't ring for you," I told her a few days ago, "just bring me up my breakfast at nine o'clock."

This morning, I have kicked off my covers. I have my eyes closed. I uncovered myself without knowing it, while asleep. When the chambermaid knocks at the door, I say "Come in!" in a dull voice. Then, as if I had only now noticed that I was uncovered, I pull up the sheets. Is it too late? I don't dare look at the chambermaid. It only adds to my embarrassment that she seems totally unmoved. A quarter of an hour later, I undertake to convince her that what just happened was accidental. I ring for her on some sort of excuse, and I stand behind the door, just showing my head, as though I did not want to be seen even in pajamas. This kind of diversion is too frequent in hotels for the chambermaid to be taken in. However, such is my gift for persuasion that she ends up saying to herself: "After all, it could be he wasn't up to any funny business."

The incident is forgotten. I invited Lucette over several times. In this way I showed that I was a normal man. For it would indeed be beyond comprehension that having so young and so pretty a mistress I be subject to such troubles.

Two weeks later I start in again. This time the chambermaid acts offended. I feign surprise at this. She gives me a piece of her mind in a fairly loud voice. Doors creep open. I shout: "What are you about to imagine!" I believe that it is difficult to be more dishonest. Once she leaves, I lock the door after her. I am shaking. It seems to me that what I have done will have terrible consequences. Then I think I can hear a voice telling me that I am not responsible. This, after he has killed, is the one the murderer must hear. Life has mistreated me. I have been so absorbed with my misfortunes that, all unawares, I have little by little ceased to mind my p's and q's. Actually, it is a good thing this incident occurred. It opened my eyes. But for it, I might have done worse later on.

The very same day I check out of the hotel.

I sit on a bench in the Tuileries, my face toward the sun. I enjoy looking at it. It is like reaching your hand out toward a fire. You withdraw your eyes the way you withdraw your hand. My thoughts turn to the future. It is obvious that this life cannot last any longer. I ask myself whether it is because of what has just taken place or because of me. I never know. An event occurs that turns our existence upside down. But if that event had not occurred! A tree hides the clock from my view. It is eleven-thirty, or noon, or half-past twelve. A stroller sits down next to me. How is it possible to disclose with such indifference so many habits, quirks, traits of character simply through one's clothes, one's gestures, the charms on one's watch chain? I compare myself to this stranger. I wish I had the help of a mirror. I wish I could see myself. I would like to know whether from looking at me one can guess who I am. Perhaps dissimulation betrays us as much as a tie-pin.

But what has got into me? I put on a scowl. I adjust it to my face and I tell myself: "I'm not scowling. This is my everyday face." I start talking to myself. My neighbor does not turn aside. A woman walks by with her child. She looks at me and she shows no surprise. I can become another man, no one will notice. My fellow creatures care very little whether I put on scowls. Once, I remember, I wanted to give myself all sorts of airs: the air of an intellectual, of an artist, of a sportsman, of a young man from a good family. Having abandoned them all, what sort of air do I have today?

I get up. Am I going to deform my movements the way I deformed my face? I alter my gait. It becomes a hippety-hop. Here comes a pretty woman. I go on hippety-hopping. After all, it may emerge that I am a native hippety-hopper. It may emerge that my hippety-hopping pleases her more than the step I normally use. I leave the Tuileries. This garden is not favorable to such exercises. You are obliged to zigzag if you are going to encounter strollers. I prefer the boulevards.

I am still the same man. I am still unable to understand the awfulness of certain comparisons. Coming straight from the most degrading intimacy, I would have fun playing with children, without wondering that their parents would leave me alone with them. I have not changed since I turn my departure from the Hôtel Maillot into an opportunity to spend a few days in Compiègne.

The weather is glacial when I arrive in that city. Stare as I will at the flowing Oise, the river seems not to be moving. Every stone, every tree is gray. Sometimes, in the final days of a season, we recapture the emotion it aroused in us at its start. You experience fresh winter sensations when, on a February morning, you land in a small city. The streets have not been cleaned because the hydrants are frozen. This neglect gives them the day-after-a-holiday look. It is ten o'clock and no one is abroad. I am a stranger. You may have lived for a long time in a city and there will still be sections of it where you have never set foot. I strike out in their direction, toward the barracks, the gasworks. Why this initial avoidance of parts that are familiar to me? Why this detour? When I used to go to Albert Dechatellux's, I would enter by a door located at the end of the garden. Thus did I seem more cordially greeted. To appear at ease, I always resorted to little tricks of this sort.

After having walked all the way around the large park, I come, by way of the forest, to the neighborhood where the avenues are. A stillness lies over the properties. Are they inhabited by the same persons? What presents itself to my view, but to my view alone, is the past. I run into a certain Doctor Fernstein whom I thought was dead. "It is with regret that we learn of the death of Dr. Fernstein of Compiègne." My eyes fell upon that obituary notice. But it was not he, since he is walking past me, unaware that I thought him to be dead. How peaceful these broad avenues are! I feel like a stranger here. A little farther on I catch sight of the town's foremost personage, a former government minister, for three decades a deputy in parliament, member of the departmental council, and mayor: Monsieur Chauvigny. He is walking along briskly. Where is he going? Being the most notable figure hereabouts, he cannot have humiliating errands to attend to. Today as in days past, he is yet on his way to the home of friends.

Why should I not pay a visit to Jacqueline? We are not enemies. She performed good works beyond what duty requires. I have no right to resent her not having done enough. I present myself at her door. What a surprise! Jacqueline is a ghost. Growing old, she has become thin. Her back is bowed. Her hair has thinned. I had no acquaintance with old age. I had never had the occasion to compare it with youth. To me it had always had the appearance of a gradual evolution. And today, as though nature had placed me outside of time, I come back to find old a person I had known young. Jacqueline is now but an elderly lady who receives me with kindness because we have both understood our errors. And when she speaks to me as if to a brother her own age, I feel that she does not understand me any better today than she did yesterday. She was thirty years old, I was ten. I gaze at her. I am still less her son now than in the past. I am just some boy she brought up and whom she lost contact with. But she, ah, she is more than my mother. She is that beautiful young woman whom unhappy children run past in order to attract attention. Denise was also that sort of woman, not for me, for other children. I remember seeing them run past. They used to wait for her, then start their little game all over again. I would have to tell them to go on home. Then I would rejoin Denise, feeling I was cruel. I had forgotten what I myself had gone through.

"What would have become of that little boy if I hadn't been there?" Jacqueline is asking herself, no doubt finding it an admirable thing that I have grown to manhood. What a strange question! Why does she not ask herself others of the same sort? "Who would I have married if I had not met Etienne? What would have happened if war hadn't broken out?"

I return to Paris. I return to where I lead my life whereas for so long I would take this same train in to Paris just for the day. For a few seconds I consider the odd-looking boulevard

Denain, so short for a street so wide. I am carrying a suitcase bought years ago in a secondhand shop. It is lined
inside with red leather. F. Best, 186 Sloane Street. It reflects
my tastes: richness and simplicity. It does however have a
stain: its origin. But that stain, does it not extend to my
whole person?

I take the bus. Former Cabinet Minister Chauvigny does
not see me. Many is the time we have made this trip together. I know he will get off at the corner of boulevard
Haussmann, rejoicing at the splendid door-to-door service
since he will have only a few steps to take in order to reach
the headquarters of I know not what corporation, whose
president he is.

I get off farther on, at Opéra. Paris may shift this way and
that but for me Opéra is still its center. I am heading toward the Louvre. I get on another bus, a little put out by
this unnecessary inconvenience of having to change.

On rue du Laos there is an hotel where I recall living at
one time. It is not until ten o'clock that I make up my
mind to go in. There is no one in sight. I take a seat in the
foyer and wait. The night-clerk comes up to me. He is
prematurely bald. That is the only thing I notice. I offer
him a cigarette. I say to him: "Let's go have a drink." It's
typical of me, this way of ingratiating myself. He accepts
provided I not take offence if he is obliged to leave. No, I
shall not take offence.

"Do you know a café?"

He looks at me in surprise.

"Sure, right across the street."

He points to an establishment before which extends an
empty terrace. Tables are pushed together, chairs stacked
upon them, all this very professionally. Through the
thicket of upright chair-legs I can make out a dim light
probably illuminating the end of the day tally. We sit down

very close to the owners, but without actually joining them. The fact of being done a favor never escapes me. I am very alive to preferential treatment and special permissions for I still remember the days when they would say to me: "Kindly oblige us by getting out of here this instant."

At the cash register they are missing two or three francs. While the husband is trying to find where the error comes from the wife is looking us over. She wears a pince-nez, has a lady-like air. Then a fifteen-year-old boy comes in from the back room. I am told he is a nephew whose father, a non-commissioned officer, fought in the Riff campaign. The youngster is in a Catholic boarding school in Sarlat, an institution for boys prone to misbehavior. I go out for a glass of beer with a night-clerk and I find out that Sarlat has a boarding school for bad boys! Then the woman talks about the *grandes écoles*. She's very eager to have her nephew go to the Naval College.

The night-clerk has been called away. I am alone. All is silence now that the mistake has been found. I think about my life. Why did not one of the charitable souls who looked after me during my youth think of sending me to Sarlat or, better yet, of enrolling me at the Naval College?

I go up to my room. It is dismally lit by one bulb of twenty-five watts at best. I set down my suitcase on a table covered with a sheet of glass under which you can see the pattern of a lace doily. The curtains have been drawn shut. The temperature is mild. There is no trace of the previous occupant, at least nothing visible. Such as it is, the room suits me. I sit on the bed. It has been turned down. I notice right away, from their plaster-like nubbliness, that the sheets are of inferior quality.

There is a knock at the door. It's my café companion, back in his night-clerk's role, who has come to ask whether I need anything. Such attention is excessive for an hotel in this category. In any case I do not respond to it. I am not sad. My lassitude is merely physical. Nothing hereabouts has anything to do with me. The table is a table. I do not even feel out of my element. It seems to me I shall never have that feeling again.

I am awakened in the middle of the night by a crying child. A woman starts singing the most mournful lullabies imaginable. My mother must have sung me to sleep with songs like that. I would have thought, a few years ago, that I was in the near vicinity of I know not what abyss of woe.

I am unable to get back to sleep. I recall that I once came into this hotel with a woman. It was in the period when now and then Denise and I would come to Paris for the day. This woman had asked me why I had picked her. She was at least fifty years old, and she had pretensions to conversation. She wanted to get me to say that in her I expected a greater flexibility. She was wrong. I simply lacked confidence in myself. I wished to create the impression that I was a well-conducted man got hold of by a professional. I truly must turn my mind to something else if I want to fall asleep. And also that mother must stop singing.

The desire Madame Vallosier aroused in me has suddenly disappeared. She believes that I have understood that she is a respectable woman. And now she wishes to exert a wholesome influence upon me. I go back to see her however. I feel that my existence is about to change and in the meantime I find it nice to live my life one day at a time.

One evening we push a sofa in front of the window and sit down side by side, as at a show. It is the first day of spring. The windows are open. The moon shines on the leafless gardens of Villa des Ternes. The children are not yet in bed. Above us other windows are open. A man is talking. He is fulminating against the government. All of a sudden he quiets down and says: "My darling." I guess him to be an older man from whom we shall not hear any disturbing language. Even so I am quaking. Finally he ceases talking. I feel rescued. But Madame Vallosier gets up abruptly, turns on the lights. No gesture shows me more clearly how far apart we are. So long as the man kept talking she felt herself safe.

I have learned that my brother André has a mistress. Like the Germaine of old she has a certain small amount of money, but she is far less of a danger than Germaine for my mother is there to supervise. She is an attorney's secretary. As she has done for the past eleven years, she goes to the office every morning. She has some savings, she has parents. From time to time, she does my mother favors. She enjoys all the advantages that come from being a long-time employee. She can fall ill, ask for an extended leave. On account of all this her private life is adorned by a certain prestige. She lives in a trim little apartment. She is ready to sacrifice everything for André, but he has his mother and demands nothing of her. Physically, she has been able to take on the appearances of a woman who spends all her time at home. She owns a single piece of jewelry, but of great value. Her mouth, which is very unattractive, is always partway open and glistening. She is unduly preoccupied with her hands. And above all has an unpleasant way of saying the word *monsieur*. She says it too often, even after a relaxed, friendly conversation. I think of that Christmas Eve when we drank champagne, when we kissed under the mistletoe, and when suddenly, as we were saying goodbye, she said to me: "Goodbye, Monsieur."

We are at my mother's, sitting opposite each other.

André has not yet come home. Am I going to tell this touchy person the following story?

Inside a rue des Acacias café I notice a stunningly beautiful woman who is paying what she owes. I halt. Rather than go in I wait for her to get up so that we shall pass one another between the tables out on the terrace. She comes out at last. Our eyes meet. At that same moment she realizes she has forgotten her gloves. She smiles at her distractedness and turns back in the direction she has come from. I step to one side to let her pass. She had been sitting at a table near the door. Since I shall still be in her way when she comes out again she invites me to go first. Then I exhibit some quick thinking. I fetch the gloves and hand them to her. "I sensed, Madame, that you'd forgotten your gloves." She smiles at me. I go on: "But I am going to inconvenience you, Madame, for I wasn't intending to enter this café." Walking abreast, we make our way between the tables. She turns her head to thank me. And in order that she preserve a good opinion of me, I move off instead of continuing to talk with her.

Is it because I find André's mistress stupid that I tell her a stupid story? Is it because I am weary of these childish performances of mine that I relate them to someone who will not excuse me for them?

Solange Vibot, Denise's friend, has been married for several years. I accidentally run into her on rue de Richelieu. We stand there and talk, obstructing the narrow sidewalk. Only inches away from us, cars stream past without interruption.

"Are you going in my direction?" she asks me.

We set off together. Never before have I been so well in command of myself.

"I haven't been to Compiègne for ages," she tells me.

"Neither have I."

My most recent trip does not count. I walk alongside Solange without looking at her. I rejoice in walking close to her side as I would with an intimate friend, with a sister. We are equals. Denise and I never were, whereas now Solange and I are. Equality is the ideal of my life. A gentle drizzle is falling. For the moment everything is perfect. No flirtatious banter. We separate without hesitation, without regret. My guess is that we shall see each other again.

Right now there is something bothering me. It is an extraordinary fact that I who have never possessed anything, I who never wanted to hold on to anything, I feel the need to be rich. How I regret having been so heedless! How well I understand the way they would cling to their possessions, the people I knew, how I understand their prudence, their wariness! It was beyond me why others took so long coming to a decision while I settled everything in the snap of a finger. Such are my thoughts as I return home, that is to say as I head for rue du Laos. Truly, there is nothing so tiresome as this need for bigger and better which invades us the moment we want to please. And these regrets! We become angry with ourselves, as with a business representative of ours who had swindled us. Had we known that we would one day love and be loved!

It is night behind the Ecole Militaire. But here is a little bit of light. Can't I be loved the way I am? We are all just human beings, some of whom are happy. Can't I number among the latter for a few years? Solange has no reason to regret the possessions I might have been able to acquire.

Two days later I telephone her. "I shall telephone," I had said when I left her. This is a disagreeable moment, smacking of my proceedings in the past. I am in the booth, alone. It is more than ever upon what I say that everything will hinge. I clack my tongue to ensure its alertness. I must feel

unconstrained, natural. In this telephone call there must
be nothing but a man's attraction toward a woman. What
great luck that I have at last found a being who awakens
authentic feelings in me! For an instant I think of telling
Solange how hard it has been for me to telephone to her.
Why do that? Why always talk about what you feel? Can I
not simply say to her that I would be very happy to see her?

"Dear friend, I would be very happy to see you."

"Do you want to have lunch together in Versailles some
day when the weather turns nice?"

"It may be several days before we get any nice weather . . ."

"Come to my studio then. I must warn you it's a mess.
I haven't been back for three years. We'll go to Versailles
some other time."

Versailles! Versailles again! Why that city is forever re-
curring in my life I simply do not know.

She will be expecting me at five o'clock. I was the one who
chose the time. I almost suggested four, or even three. I
subdue my impatience. It's a victory to add to those I have
been winning these past few weeks.

But here is a defeat. I am the only customer in a dimly lit
room of a small café on rue du Cherche-Midi, a five-minute
walk from rue Falguière, near the military prison, to be
exact. I still cannot resist making a stop in a café prior to a
rendezvous. Starting this morning I could tell that this
meeting would occupy my thoughts well before the time
set for it to begin. "I'll go have a coffee in the neighborhood." And so here I am, sitting upon this shallow wall-
sofa, here and there swollen by a spring that has come
loose. The owner is wearing a herringbone woolen vest. If
Richard were wearing it, would not this vest look as if it
came from a clothier of the first order? It is with such stuff

I busy my mind. I am brought the mighty cup of coffee I have been planning to drink since this morning and for which I have no desire. All I had to do was just stay in my hotel. All I had to do was while the time away, whatever that might have taken, and then leave at the last moment, even if I arrived ten minutes late. But why choose a small, dark, out of the way café? Why not go to boulevard Montparnasse? Was I afraid of some incident preventing me from joining Solange? Was I afraid of running into her before the time we had arranged?

At last the hour is at hand. On rue de Sèvres I walk past a hospital. I avoid glancing at the signs announcing office hours. Here is rue Falguière. While walking I have tried to visualize the studio. It does not at all resemble the sort of one-room apartment I had imagined. It is a place outfitted for work. Upon the wall, no El Greco "Christ", no Botticelli "Spring" as at her place on rue du Château-d'Eau, but rarer reproductions. I look at them attentively, slightly embarrassed to be unacquainted with them. The studio is lit by one large frosted glass light-bulb. Solange, who is preparing tea, invites me to take a seat. A padded Louis XV armchair here? A piece of furniture serving as a pretext for jokes? But I keep still.

Two days later I do not leave my room until I set out for our new rendezvous. All day long I had the impression I was a man who wore glasses only when at home. No one sees him. He works a bit at this, a bit at that. And then he takes off his glasses, he is going to step out.

We are sitting at an outdoor table at the Dôme, side by side, in the broad sunshine, amid a crowd of customers. Certain passers-by gaze at us. It seems to me that they are standing still, that we are the ones who are moving. We do not look at each other, Solange and I. I would like to declare exactly what I am, be loved because I hide nothing.

For a woman, what I am hiding is far less serious than a disease. How I dreaded them, those diseases that might prevent me from loving!

I look for Solange. The weather is radiant: a spring morning. I pay no attention at all to the handsome qualities of the building, to the aspect of the avenue. I am almost indifferent to appearances and the feeling this gives me is a feeling of great well being. How far away are the observations I would have made if Denise were alive!

At last Solange appears. She stops in front of the concierges' lodge and says a few words. How pleasant it is to watch orders being given! Smiling, she walks toward me. No longer am I minded to stand back. I walk up to meet her. At this instant there is nothing I am reproaching myself for.

We continue on foot as far as the Gare des Invalides. As we cross the Esplanade, I am reminded of certain shameful acts. With Solange at my side I walk past the benches and hidden nooks which evoke them. The station is almost deserted. Solange frightens me a little. She strays off, she follows me. We climb up into an empty compartment. It is an old train, for it is eleven o'clock in the morning, one of those old trains they run between the rush hours. Twenty years ago all the trains were like this. It makes me think of the ideal life I used to dream about. Those departures, on a weekday, during slack hours, that relief at the absence of a crowd to follow, that joy in the enjoyment of organizations temporarily asleep, those lunches when everyone has left, for which the restaurant personnel come back to life! I know how to make myself liked by people for whom I am the cause of extra work.

"Solange, I find you charming!"

She smiles. She accepts that I find her charming. She

even accepts being told so by a man like me. I think of those who know who I am. If they spoke, would Solange listen to them?

The train has started. We are alone. The Seine flows inside the mists. And now Paris is retreating into the distance. Oh! how different this Paris is from the one I so often discovered on coming back from Compiègne. The Eiffel Tower no longer hides its legs from us. The houses on the right bank contemplate the same panorama we do.

We have arrived. Wide avenues such as they have in Compiègne, movie posters where the typography is already that used in provincial newspapers. Planes fly in the blue sky, so much higher than in the old days. For an instant the breeze brings their drone to us. What a sad sound! I would so like to leave! I would so like to be still happier! I would so like not to be thinking about my mother's sister, that woman who worked as a servant, I believe, for a family in Versailles!

It is half-past two. We are in a restaurant. The day is already over, and yet the sun is still shining in the sky. How I would desire something else! How I would desire that the oncoming evening be as beautiful as the morning; that there be no liqueur glasses on the table, no cigarette smoke in this little dining room! How I would desire that we be more forthright, that we not be two people in love, that Solange's face not be flushed! Her hands, which I have looked at perhaps one hundred times without thinking about them, are motionless at present. I would like to kiss them. I talk. Solange talks. But why can I not prevent myself from thinking that this moment is but a minute in my life? Why does a voice whisper in my ear that we are only two, that even if we love each other we shall still be only two?

Resting my hands on the table, I work round it. I sit

down beside Solange. I did not straighten up in order to change place. I wanted to give Solange the illusion I have wound up next to her without having moved. Our arms touch. We have been together since morning. We have lived near to one another for years without being acquainted. I take Solange's hand. She does not lower her eyes.

I go back to rue du Laos. I need to know where I am headed. I kissed Solange at the end of our lunch. Indeed, these love affairs pursued in restaurants have the hallmark of gluttony. I perform gestures that are forever the same. This existence cannot last any longer. There is one thing I am sure of. If a new war were to break out, I would be a hero this time or I would be killed. But there will be no war. I will not be a hero, and I will not be killed. I am forty-one years old. What am I going to do? The impossibility of answering this question does not dishearten me. I feel that an event (I have been feeling it for several months) is going to occur in my life, some unforeseen and extraordinary event. Without the slightest doubt I shall then write the sequel to these memoirs. I can here and now declare that it will be so different from the beginning that my future readers simply will not be able to believe it was written by the same man.

June, 1939

DATE DUE
